THE STOLEN SPARKLER

PREQUEL TO THE

LADY ROSALYND AND STEELE MYSTERIES

MAGDA ALEXANDER

CHAPTER 1

December 1888
Yorkshire, England

LADY ROSALYND

"MUST YOU GO, ROSIE?" Petunia's tearful voice quivered as she buried her face in my gown. No surprise that the fabric was quickly dampened by her flood of tears.

Her grief was not entirely unexpected. After our parents had been tragically killed six years ago, I'd taken on the role of caretaker for my siblings, a responsibility I wore proudly. For all intents and purposes, I was the only mother Petunia had ever known, and each parting, no matter how brief, felt monumental to her. So it was no surprise she dreaded a separation.

I crouched down to Petunia's level, gently lifting my sister's chin so I could look into her eyes. "I'll only be gone for three days, poppet," I soothed, brushing a stray copper curl from her tear-streaked cheek. "I promise I'll return in time for Sunday service. I'll be but ten miles away at Lady Eleanor's home, barely a two-hour drive. If something dire occurs, Cosmos can send word, and I'll return at once."

Petunia sniffed, her small lips trembling. "But what if something happens to *you*?"

I chuckled softly, placing a kiss on her forehead. "Nothing will happen to me, my sweet. The roads from here to Lady Eleanor's home are well maintained, and no snow is expected."

Logical as my arguments were, she was not about to concede her grievance. "But what if a highwayman accosts you?"

I arched a brow. "A highwayman? Who put that thought in your head?"

Laurel's cheeks turned bright red. My twelve-year-old sister loved to read novels, the more lurid the better. I tried to hide them, as they were not proper reading materials for her, but she always managed to find them in our vast library. But now was not the time to call her out on it. Not when Petunia's concern needed to be addressed. In as kind a voice as I could manage, I said, "There are no highwaymen in Yorkshire, sweetheart."

"But—"

The grandfather clock in the drawing room chimed, reminding me of the hour. "No more, poppet. I have to leave. I promised Eleanor I'd arrive at Needham Hall before luncheon. You don't want me to disappoint her, do you?"

She sniffed once more. "No."

"You'll be in good hands here with Chrissie." My next younger sister dearly loved Petunia, indeed all of her siblings. I could rely on her to care for them. "And Cosmos as well."

Petunia scoffed. "Cosmos spends all his time with his plants. He hardly knows I exist."

Our oldest brother, the Earl of Rosehaven, was an avowed botanist who spent an inordinate amount of time in his greenhouse. But then, it was for a good reason. He'd become such an expert in British flora, Scotland Yard regularly consulted him when a thorny problem arose.

"I might starve," Petunia insisted in dramatic fashion.

"I doubt that, Petunia," Laurel said. "He shows up for all his meals, so he's bound to notice if you weren't eating."

Chrissie curled an arm around Petunia's shoulders. "I'll make sure you don't starve, sweetheart. I'll ask Cook to bake plenty of fairy cakes just for you." Fairy cakes were Petunia's favorites.

That brightened up Petunia to no end. "Promise?"

"Promise."

I smiled at Chrissie, grateful for her effort, though I knew my absence would be harder on her than she let on.

Glancing once more at the gathered group in front of the drawing room hearth, I addressed my sisters with a reassuring nod, "I expect you to be on your best behavior while I'm away. That means no teasing Petunia and no arguing with Chrissie. While I'm gone, she'll be in charge. Understood?"

The twins Holly and Ivy exchanged mischievous glances, but answered "Understood," readily enough.

"It's not fair." Laurel, ever the rebel, piped up.

"What's not fair?"

"We get admonished while our brothers are not even here to say goodbye."

"Of course, we're here," Cosmos said, entering the drawing room with William and Fox in his wake. "We couldn't very well let Rosie leave without saying goodbye." He strolled over to me and kissed my cheek. "Enjoy yourself, sister. Don't worry about them. I'll make sure they don't set themselves on fire or poison anyone."

I laughed. "Well, that's reassuring."

"Have a grand time, Rosie," William said. My strapping twenty-two-year-old brother had been traveling on the continent but, thankfully, had come home for the holidays. No one was happier than me. I had missed him dreadfully.

"I plan to."

Fox, the youngest male in the family, bowed and held out a bloom. "I cultivated it for you."

A red rose in winter. "Why that's lovely, Fox. Thank you," I said accepting the bloom. "I shall treasure it."

As I kissed his cheek, he blushed.

"Do try to care for each other until I return," I said taking them all in.

"We will," they said in unison.

Another fresh wave of tears from Petunia brought my attention back to her. "I don't want you to go," Petunia whispered.

I knelt again, pulling her into my arms for one final embrace. "I know, darling. But I promise you, I'll be back before you know it. And while I'm gone, you must be brave. Can you do that for me?"

Petunia nodded reluctantly, though her tears continued to fall.

"That's my girl," I murmured, pressing a kiss to the top of her head. "I'll see you soon."

Chrissie gently took Petunia's hand and pulled her away from my tear-stained gown. As much as my heart ached, it was time to leave.

After a final glance at my brothers and sisters, who stood in a loose formation by the hearth, I squared my shoulders and made my way to the front steps of Rosehaven Manor. Outside, the family's grand carriage awaited, its horses stamping impatiently in the cool morning air. The crisp scent of frost clung to the breeze, signaling the approach of winter, though the promise of holiday festivities softened the bite of the chill.

As I ascended into the carriage to join my maid, Tilly, I allowed myself a small sigh of contentment. The prospect of spending three days in the company of my dearest friend, Lady Eleanor Needham, free from the constant demands of managing Rosehaven Manor and its occupants, filled me with anticipation.

"Everything is packed nice and tight, milady," Tilly said, "including your ball gown."

"Thank you, Tilly." I pressed her hand. "I know I can count on you to do everything right."

"Ta, Lady Rosalynd."

Once I'd settled into the plush velvet seat of the carriage, our coachman sprung the horses. Soon, the sprawling grounds of Rosehaven Manor began to fall away, replaced by the quiet rolling hills and bare trees that lined the road to Needham Hall. The countryside, though cold and stark in its winter dress, offered a peaceful retreat from the noise and activity that typically filled my days.

As the carriage rattled along the path, I allowed myself to drift into thought. The image of Petunia's tear-streaked face lingered in my mind, tugging at my heart. My departure had unsettled my younger sister more than usual. It wasn't the first time I'd felt the sting of guilt when leaving my siblings behind. As much as I longed for moments of freedom, for a chance to be simply Rosalynd rather than a caretaker, I couldn't escape the deep sense of responsibility I felt toward my family.

But Lady Eleanor had been insistent. "You need a break, Rosalynd," she'd said just last week over tea during her fortnightly visit. "You've been running Rosehaven singlehandedly for years. Let someone else take care of things for a few days. Come to my Christmas ball—no children, no responsibilities, just good company and a chance to enjoy yourself."

The invitation had been impossible to refuse, especially when Eleanor had added with a sly smile, "Besides, I have something special planned for the ball. You won't want to miss it."

Eleanor had refused to divulge any further details. So, of course, my curiosity had been piqued. Whatever my friend had in store, it was sure to be something grand.

As the countryside passed in a blur outside the carriage window, I imagined the warmth of the firelit halls of Needham Hall, the sound of laughter and music, and the rich scent of evergreens and spices filling the air. Lady Eleanor's holiday gatherings were always a welcome reprieve from the strictures of society, and I was eager to bask in the comfort of my friend's lively household.

At some point in the journey, I dozed off. So it seemed like only minutes later I was being roused by a soft knock on the carriage door. Gazing out the window, I realized we'd arrived at Needham Hall. After our footman opened it with a slight bow, I stepped down. The cold air bit at my cheeks as I gazed up at the grand manor before me.

The sprawling estate stood majestic against the backdrop of crisp December skies, its roof and eaves dusted with frost. The manor's imposing façade was softened by the festive decorations strewn across its stone walls—evergreen garlands adorned with holly, red ribbons, and gleaming baubles. The scent of pine lingered in the cold air, mingling with the faint aroma of wood smoke curling from the chimneys. It was a scene of holiday cheer, as warm as the heart of the Christmas season.

A growing sense of happiness filled me as I gazed with wonder at the sight. What would the next four days bring? Much more than I expected, as it turned out.

CHAPTER 2

AN UNWELCOME SURPRISE

"ROSALYND!" Lady Eleanor Needham called out as she descended the front steps, her rich burgundy gown swirling in the cool breeze. A beaming smile lit her features, but the moment she grasped my hands, the slight tremor in Eleanor's fingers and the tightness around her eyes informed me something was not quite right.

I'd known Eleanor since childhood, and the bond we shared was one of deep friendship. She'd always been the picture of poise, but today she was troubled.

I didn't let on, however, that something seemed amiss. If it were particularly troublesome, she would share it with me soon enough. In the meantime, I could praise her efforts. "I've been so looking forward to this weekend, Eleanor," I said warmly. "Needham Hall looks perfectly splendid. It's clear you've worked hard on making it just so." Eleanor's father, Lord Needham, was a widower who depended on

Eleanor for the running of the household. Although they had an excellent housekeeper and staff, it fell on Eleanor to prepare the manor for the Christmas festivities. Maybe this year, it had proven too much for her.

Lady Eleanor's smile faltered as she ushered me inside. "Thank you, dear friend. I'm so glad you're here." Her voice held a note of panic.

As we ascended the grand staircase, passing servants who bustled about, putting finishing touches on the lavish decorations in the great hall, the tension in the air grew more palpable with each step we took. My mind raced as I wondered what might be troubling my friend.

Once we reached her bedroom and Eleanor closed the door behind us, the façade crumbled. Her face contorted with sudden anguish as she threw herself into my arms with a sob.

My instincts had been right. Something was seriously wrong. "Eleanor, sweetheart, whatever is the matter?" I asked, guiding my distraught friend to the edge of her bed.

For a moment, Eleanor struggled to speak, her voice trembling with emotion. "Rosalynd, it's—it's gone. The necklace is gone."

My brow furrowed in confusion. "What necklace?"

Eleanor wiped away her tears and inhaled deeply, steadying herself. "My great-great—oh, I can't remember how many—great-grandmother's diamond necklace. The one gifted to her by King Charles II. It's the most valuable thing our family owns, Rosalynd. And now, it's vanished."

Oh, dear heaven! My mind began to race. The diamond necklace was a piece of history, a priceless heirloom that carried the legacy of the Needham family. Its loss wasn't just a matter of sentimental value—it was a disaster.

"How long has it been missing?" I asked, slipping into my familiar role as a problem solver.

"I—I discovered it was gone this morning," Eleanor confessed, her voice still shaky. "I went to check on it, just to ensure everything was perfect for the Christmas Ball. You know how important the necklace is—it's tradition to wear it on special occasions. The ball will be in three days and... well, you see..."

I pressed her hands. "Please, Eleanor. Tell me."

Eleanor's hesitation was brief, but it was enough to make me sit up straighter. Eleanor glanced toward the window, her expression one of pained uncertainty, before finally continuing.

"My engagement to Stephen, Lord Cumberforth, is to be announced at the ball."

I blinked in surprise. "Engagement?" I had known Eleanor and Cumberforth were growing closer, but an engagement was a far more serious development.

Eleanor nodded, wringing her hands nervously. "Yes, but it's... complicated. Stephen's father, the Marquis of Burkett, is against the match."

My thoughts immediately shifted, piecing together the tension I had sensed from the moment I arrived. "Because he wants his son to marry someone else," I guessed, lacing my voice with understanding.

Eleanor's eyes widened slightly, impressed but not surprised by my quick intuition. "Yes, precisely. The marquis had arranged for Stephen to marry Lady Annabel Bingham, a wealthy heiress. Apparently, the Cumberforth estate is in dire need of funds, and a marriage to Lady Annabel would provide a much-needed infusion of cash."

"And without the necklace," I continued, my mind already processing the implications, "you fear Lord Burkett will use its disappearance as proof that you would bring nothing of value to the marriage."

Eleanor's breath hitched as she nodded. "I do have a

dowry, but it pales in comparison to Lady Annabel's. If I don't wear the necklace at the ball, Lord Burkett will see it as a sign of weakness. He's already looking for reasons to dissolve the engagement before it's officially announced. I've tried to explain to Stephen that we can face this together, but he's under so much pressure from his father. I fear if we don't find the necklace in time, he might"—she gulped—"he might reconsider the engagement."

"Who knows about the engagement?"

"Other than Lord and Lady Burkett? Father, of course, and now you."

"What about the rest of your family?" I knew she had several cousins as well as one aunt and two uncles.

"I kept it from them as I wanted the announcement to be a surprise at the ball."

Feeling the depth of her distress, I placed a comforting hand on Eleanor's shoulder. "Don't worry. We'll find the necklace before the ball begins." I didn't know how I would make good on my promise given we only had three days. But I would do my best to make it so. "But first, I need to know more. When was the last time you saw it?"

Eleanor took a moment to gather her thoughts. "Yesterday. I asked my maid to fetch it from my father's safe as I wanted to make sure the clasp was secured and see how it looked with my ball gown. Unfortunately, she had just slipped it around my neck when Lavinia and Felicity barged in unannounced."

"So, your cousins saw it."

"Yes. They fell into raptures over its beauty. They'd never seen it, as the necklace is only worn at weddings and engagements. I was mortified, to say the least, but tried to put on a pleasant face. After a few minutes, I asked Martha to tuck it back in the jewelry box in my dressing room, which I locked after my cousins left. This morning, when I asked Martha to

THE STOLEN SPARKLER

return the necklace to the safe . . . it was gone." Covering her face, she dissolved into tears.

I couldn't blame her. I'd feel the same way myself. "Was there any sign of tampering?" I asked in as soft a tone as I could manage.

Eleanor shook her head. "None. The jewelry box was locked, and the key was in its usual place. I don't understand how the necklace was taken."

One obvious suspect clearly stood out. "Does your maid know where you keep the key?"

"No. I ask Martha to leave the room whenever I open and lock the jewelry box." She pointed toward a nearby shelf. "I keep the key inside that vase."

Not a safe place. The maid could have easily figured it out. Even as I pondered that thought, my mind raced with possibilities. "Who else knew about the necklace?"

Eleanor bit her lip. "Besides my cousins? The servants. It's common knowledge as it's part of the family lore. But none of the staff would have taken it," she asserted. "They are loyal to the core!"

Even a loyal servant could be tempted to steal a valuable piece of jewelry. But it wouldn't do to suspect any of them until I had more facts. "Who else arrived before I did?"

She blushed. "Stephen. He arrived shortly after my cousins."

"What about your aunt and uncles?"

"Uncle Martin won't be here until Saturday. Uncle Wilford has a chest complaint, so neither he nor my aunt will be attending." She didn't seem particularly upset about their absence. I, on the other hand, rejoiced. It meant there would be fewer suspects.

I paused to consider her words. Stephen could be a possible suspect. Maybe the pressure from his father had become too much for him, and he'd settled on this strategy to cry off from his engagement. It had not been made public after all. Only Eleanor, her father, and now I, knew. It would be an easy thing to end an engagement that, in the eyes of the world, had never begun. It was an interesting theory I would need to explore.

"What about the staff?" I asked. "Has anyone new been hired recently?"

Eleanor nodded slowly. "We took on a new housemaid last month. Her name is Lucy. But . . . I can't believe she would be involved. She's been so diligent and sweet."

I filed that information away for later. "I'll need to speak to her, just to be thorough." Indeed, I would need to talk to the entire staff. The idea seemed daunting given the short time frame we had.

"I don't want to accuse anyone unfairly," Eleanor whispered, wringing her hands.

I squeezed her shoulder gently. "We won't. But we must be methodical if we're to solve this."

I came to my feet as my mind whirled with potential leads, possibilities, and questions. The missing necklace, the looming engagement announcement, the Marquis of Burkett's disapproval, the new housemaid—it was all connected somehow. And time was of the essence. The ball was but a few days away.

Eleanor nodded, her hope returning with the certainty in my voice. "Thank you, Rosalynd. I don't know what I'd do without you."

I smiled softly, my mind already calculating the next steps. "We'll find it. And you will wear that necklace on Saturday. Mark my words."

Needham Hall, with all its festive cheer, was now a stage for a growing intrigue. I had little time, but I would uncover the truth. The necklace was the key to Eleanor's future—and I would not allow it to slip away without a fight.

CHAPTER 3

THE DUKE'S ARRIVAL

THE EARLY MORNING MIST clung to Needham Hall as my carriage rolled up the gravel drive. The reason for my presence was a rather simple one. Needham had summoned me here to discuss a measure that would soon come before the House of Lords.

In recent weeks, my mind had been consumed with political matters. So many, they had commandeered my life. You'd think I would wish to avoid more of the same. But strangely enough, I'd found myself anticipating this weekend. Why? I had no idea. Maybe it was the pleasure of seeing an old friend. He didn't visit London often enough.

But even if I'd wished to cry off, I wouldn't have done so. I couldn't say no to Needham, not after everything the man had done for me. Years ago, in the wake of a deeply personal tragedy, Needham pulled me back from the brink of despair. The debt I owed him was one I could never fully repay.

As the carriage came to a halt, my valet, Roberts, leapt

down to open the door. As I stepped out, my eyes took in the array of festive decorations adorning the manor's façade. Garlands of holly and ivy were draped along the railings, wreaths adorned with scarlet ribbons hung on every door, and the scent of pine lingered in the crisp air. Years past, I would've enjoyed such a vision, not so much anymore.

A footman appeared from within the manor to escort me inside. I followed him without delay, my strides purposeful as I crossed the threshold into the great hall. The manor bustled with activity as servants rushed about to complete preparations for the upcoming Christmas Ball. Yet, even amidst the hustle, something felt off. The energy in the air was strained, as though a shadow had fallen over the household.

"Your Grace, this way," the footman said. Acknowledging his prompt, I followed him through a series of corridors toward the familiar room I'd visited more than once—Needham's study.

As I entered the space, I found my old friend standing by the hearth, gazing into the crackling fire.

"Needham," I greeted him, in a calm and steady voice.

The earl turned, his face pale and drawn while offering a weak smile. "Steele. Thank you for coming."

The Earl of Needham was not a man easily rattled, and the sight of him looking so deeply troubled set off alarm bells in my mind.

As I clasped my friend's hand, my gaze scanned his features. "You look as though you've seen a ghost. What's happened?"

Needham sighed, running a hand through his graying hair. "I intended this weekend to be one of joy and celebration, but this morning has brought . . . complications."

"Complications?" I would need more than that.

Needham nodded as he moved to his desk, where a glass

of brandy sat untouched. After he gestured for me to sit, he leaned heavily against the edge of the furnishing. "It's Eleanor's necklace. The family heirloom—the diamond necklace that was given to an ancestress of mine by Charles II. It's gone. Stolen."

I narrowed my gaze. "Stolen? How so?"

"We discovered the theft this morning. Eleanor was planning to wear the necklace on Saturday at the ball to mark her engagement to Lord Cumberforth. That's to be kept a secret for now. But when she checked her jewelry box this morning, it was missing."

"The engagement was to be announced Saturday?" I asked, my mind already turning over the possibilities.

Needham let out a humorless chuckle. "Yes, provided the necklace is found. Lord Cumberforth's father, the Marquis of Burkett, already disapproves of the match. If the necklace isn't found, it will be another strike against Eleanor. The marquis has made it no secret that he wishes his son to marry a wealthy heiress, not a young woman who, by his estimation, brings little to the table."

My thoughts sharpened. "Burkett would have something to gain from the necklace remaining lost, then. And the timing of this theft . . . just before the engagement announcement. It's suspicious."

Needham nodded wearily. "Yes, but he has an unimpeachable alibi. He hasn't arrived."

"He wouldn't have performed the deed himself. He's too clever for that. No, he would have arranged for another person to do the task. But one can't accuse a man of theft without proof. Burkett is no fool. If he's behind this, he's covered his tracks well."

I paused for a measured length as I considered the situation. My expertise in matters of investigation—especially those concerning delicate political and social entanglements—was well known in certain circles. It was why Needham had subtly mentioned the theft to me now. The earl wasn't asking directly, but his unspoken plea for help was clear.

"I'll help you, Needham," I said finally. "I'll look into the matter."

The earl's relief was palpable. "Thank you, Steele. I knew I could count on you."

"Do you have any leads?" I asked.

"None so far," Needham admitted. "Although Eleanor discovered the theft this morning, she believes the necklace was taken yesterday afternoon or evening. She can't fathom how it happened. The jewelry box was locked, and there was no sign of forced entry."

"Have you questioned the staff?"

"Not yet. I was waiting until you arrived before taking on that task. I would hate to think any one of them has taken it."

"Understandably so." I would feel the same. A man was entitled to feel he could trust his staff. "Which guests have arrived?" I inquired.

"Lord Cumberforth arrived yesterday afternoon, as did several of my nieces and nephews. And Eleanor welcomed Lady Rosalynd, Rosehaven's sister, this morning after the necklace had gone missing."

I arched a brow at the mention of Lady Rosalynd's name. "Lady Rosalynd? She's here?"

Needham offered a faint smile. "Yes. Eleanor's oldest and dearest friend. Do you know her?"

"Not an acquaintance, but I do know her by name and sight. The Rosehaven London residence is situated on Grosvenor Square."

"Same as yours."

I nodded. "But we belong to different circles. She has a reputation as a social reformer."

"Not a priority of yours," Needham said, somewhat amused.

"No," I agreed. My particular interest in the House of Lords was the security of the nation and everyone who resided within. "We'll need to speak to everyone who was in the house since yesterday afternoon. Servants and family—no one can be excluded."

Before Needham could respond, the door to the study burst open without so much as a knock. Lady Eleanor, her face a study in anguish, stood in the doorway with Lady Rosalynd close behind her.

"Father, we—oh!" Eleanor stopped short, her eyes widening as she spotted me.

"Steele, you know my daughter, Eleanor."

I came to my feet, "Of course. A pleasure to see you again."

"And the other young lady is Lady Rosalynd, Rosehaven's sister."

I'd only seen her from a distance across Grosvenor Square. She couldn't be missed. Her hair, a shocking shade of copper, had always caught my attention. What I had never been close enough to appreciate was the perfection of her face. Porcelain skin, a bloom of pink on her cheeks, and eyes a striking shade of blue. After a brief hesitation, I advanced and bowed over her hand. "A pleasure to make your acquaintance, Lady Rosalynd."

"Your Grace." Her curtsy was everything it should be. Her expression was not. There was a hint of aggravation in her gaze. Clearly, she was not pleased to see me.

But I had no chance to wonder about it as Needham was coming to his feet. "Anything wrong, Eleanor?" His voice held a tone of alarm as if he was expecting yet more bad news.

"No. I'm sorry to interrupt, Father," Eleanor began, her

voice shaking slightly. "But Rosalynd and I have been discussing my missing necklace, and—" she hesitated, glancing at her friend for support.

Rosalynd stepped forward, her expression resolute. "I've offered to help investigate its disappearance, Lord Needham. Eleanor is beside herself with worry. I believe I may be able to assist in finding the necklace."

Needham's eyes flickered with surprise, but before he could respond, I cleared my throat. "Lady Rosalynd," I said, slightly inclining my head. "You intend to investigate?"

Her unflinching sharp blue eyes met mine. "Yes, Your Grace. I have experience in solving such matters."

I suppressed a smile. Lady Rosalynd Rosehaven may very well have many talents, but the idea of her successfully conducting an investigation into a theft of this magnitude seemed . . . improbable, especially given the short amount of time to be had. This was no drawing-room mystery but a matter of serious consequence.

Still, I was not one to dismiss anyone's abilities outright. She had a determined look in her eye, and perhaps there was some merit to her involvement—if only to keep her occupied while I conducted the real investigation.

Needham must have sensed the tension between us because he quickly intervened. "The duke has graciously agreed to assist us as well. I was just asking for his help before you arrived."

Rosalynd's lips pressed into a thin line. "I . . . see." She appeared none too pleased with that suggestion, but then she recovered quickly enough. "Perhaps we should work together, Your Grace."

I raised an eyebrow, surprised by her response. "Together?"

"Yes." Needham seized on the suggestion. "It would be better if the two of you joined forces. Lady Rosalynd has a unique perspective, and you, Steele, have your own . . . expertise. Between the two of you, I believe we can solve this before Saturday's ball."

I wasn't so sure about that, but it was clear Needham wanted Lady Rosalynd to be involved. And after everything he'd done for me, how could I refuse?

"Very well," I agreed, though my tone remained doubtful. "We'll work as a team."

Lady Rosalynd's eyes flashed with amusement. Seemingly, she'd correctly interpreted my hesitation. "How very gracious of Your Grace," she said, amusement clear in her voice. "With your . . . expertise, and my unique perspective, we're sure to find the necklace in no time."

I bit back a retort. What else could I do? I was bound to Needham by friendship and duty, and now I was bound to Lady Rosalynd as well—though how much help she would be remained to be seen.

CHAPTER 4

QUESTIONING THE STAFF

AFTER THAT TENSE MEETING in Lord Needham's study, we proceeded to the dining room where our luncheon was being served. Eleanor's cousins, as well as Lord Cumberforth, were all present. Having met them before, I knew what to expect.

I quickly found my name card, located between Alistair, one of Eleanor's cousins, and Lord Cumberforth. No doubt Eleanor had chosen that seating arrangement to keep her female cousins from vexing her fiancé. I, on the other hand, would say nothing to irritate him. It would not be a difficult thing to accomplish.

As the son of a marquis, Lord Cumberforth could have been a vain, pompous sort of man, especially given his father's arrogance. But the gentleman was kind and unassuming. And most importantly, clearly in love with Eleanor evidenced by the warmth in his gaze whenever it lighted on her. A sentiment she fully reciprocated.

Eleanor, the very definition of an English rose with her dark ringlets and fair complexion, had received many offers of marriage since her debut. But she'd held out for a love match. Clearly, she'd found it in him. Striking him off my list of suspects, I vowed to do whatever was needed to ensure she got her heart's desire.

Unfortunately, the fond glances exchanged between Eleanor and Cumberforth did not go unnoticed by Eleanor's cousin, Miss Lavinia Needham. Similar in coloring to Eleanor's she was known for her penchant for gossip. "A little birdie told me to expect an announcement this weekend," she hinted with a smirk. "Care to share what that could be, Eleanor?"

"I'm afraid you've been misinformed," Eleanor asserted, tearing her smitten gaze away from her fiancé.

Lavinia pruned her lips. "Oh?" That simple word communicated pure skepticism. She didn't believe Eleanor for a moment.

"Stop teasing Eleanor," her brother Alastair said in a pleasant voice. "She's not going to reveal anything. At least not before it's time." He winked at Eleanor.

I did not wonder why he wished to remain in Eleanor's and, by extension, her father's good graces. Needham had no male issue, which meant one day Alistair would inherit the Needham title and estate. He was easygoing and affable, though not particularly inclined toward serious conversation. As he enjoyed a passion for horses and outdoor sports, he preferred the stables and the playing fields. Still, he was more than happy to attend family events, especially when they were held at Needham Hall.

"Honestly, Lavinia. What a busybody you are," Miss Felicity Needham, Eleanor's other female cousin, chided. The daughter of Lord Needham's youngest brother, she neither enjoyed Eleanor's beauty nor Lavinia's liveliness. As she stood to inherit nothing, her goal was to marry and marry well, something she'd pursued since her debut. Much as she tried, she'd found that goal difficult to accomplish. And at twenty-eight years of age, she was growing desperate. "I find it downright rude to inquire about someone's marriage plans. Especially, when they may never come to pass." Turning to the duke who was seated next to her, she asked, "Don't you agree, Your Grace?"

It was no wonder she was seeking favor with Steele. She probably thought of him as a prospect, given he was a widower. I knew nothing about the duke's views on walking down the aisle once more. But since he hadn't done so for close to ten years after his wife's death, it was logical to assume he was not in the market for a spouse. But then again, what did I know?

"I find it best to keep my opinions to myself, Miss Needham," Steele said. A response that could be taken in many ways. But then, he was known for his circumspect remarks.

Felicity must have decided he'd agreed with her as she let out a cackling laugh. "Your Grace, how very marvelous you joined us for the Christmas Ball festivities. I fully intend to ensure you enjoy yourself."

"A noble sentiment," Steele said.

The remainder of the luncheon continued pleasantly enough. Alistair proved to be an amusing conversationalist, as long as he was allowed to discuss his beloved horseflesh. As for Cumberforth, I only exchanged brief remarks with him as his eyes and ears were all for Eleanor.

At the end of the meal, Eleanor announced she'd planned an outing for this afternoon—a trip to the woods to fetch the Yule log for the cavernous fireplace in the hall. The duke excused himself from the activity as there was something he needed to attend to. I claimed I needed to lie down as a migraine was making itself felt.

Amidst a chorus of "Hope you feel better," and "Get your rest," I made my exit alongside the duke. He was solicitous enough to offer his arm while we climbed the stairs before we headed to our respective bedchambers. We'd previously decided we'd meet in the study once the Yule log party departed Needham Hall.

I didn't have long to wait. Fifteen minutes later, there was a knock on my door. Eleanor's maid, Martha, stood on the other side. "They've gone, milady."

"Thank you, Martha."

The house was a maze of narrow hallways, dark wooden paneling, and plush carpets—familiar and yet suddenly unfamiliar in the light of what had occurred. There was no need to rush. I did, however, as I didn't want to keep the duke waiting. He'd made it perfectly clear he thought me a lightweight. My pride refused to confirm that opinion by being late. I arrived at the study to find the duke already there, his back to the fireplace.

Curtsying, I said, "Your Grace, I hope I didn't keep you waiting."

"Not at all." He inclined his head. "I arrived but a minute ago."

I had to admit he made an imposing figure in his perfectly tailored garments. There was nothing of the dandy about him, however. More than likely, he simply appreciated a well-cut cloth. Tall and broad-shouldered with a streak of white in his black hair—a family trait I'd heard—he commanded the room in a way that did not seem possible. And yet he did. As always, he was dressed in unrelenting black. According to rumors, it signified mourning for his wife, who'd died during childbirth barely a year into their marriage.

"First things first," he began briskly, his hands clasped

behind his back. "We need to establish the timeline. When did Lady Eleanor first realize the necklace was stolen?"

After taking a seat on the settee closest to the fireplace, I replied, "This morning. She opened her jewelry box to make certain the necklace was there, only to find it gone."

The duke nodded thoughtfully. "Who knew where the necklace was kept?"

"Her maid," I answered. "The necklace is usually kept in Lord Needham's safe here in his study, but yesterday she asked her maid to fetch it. She wanted to make sure the clasp was secure, and the stones were polished. And she wanted to see how it looked with her ball gown."

"Who was in the house at the time?" The duke's gaze was piercing, his expression unyielding.

I recited the list Eleanor and I had pieced together. "All the servants, naturally. Lady Eleanor's cousins. Lord Cumberforth arrived shortly after them. His parents are expected to arrive tomorrow."

"Did the cousins see the necklace?"

I hesitated. "Her female cousins did. She was wearing it when they came into her room. It's possible they told their brothers about it. They're a close-knit family."

"A dangerous thing, flaunting such a valuable piece," he muttered.

I rushed to her defense. "She wasn't flaunting it. They showed up unannounced."

"Ummm." That supercilious brow of his took a hike. "Regardless, we'll need to follow up on that. But first I need to inspect Lady Eleanor's bedchamber. We have to determine if there was any sign of forced entry or if the thief entered by more subtle means."

I inclined my head in agreement. "Yes, of course. Martha, her maid, is waiting there for us." Eleanor had arranged it during our previous discussion.

Lost in thought, I held my silence while we climbed the stairs and proceeded to Eleanor's bedchamber. Martha was expecting us as we barely had to knock before she thrust open the door. "Your Grace, milady," After a brief curtsy, she moved aside.

Once inside Eleanor's room, the duke and I surveyed the surroundings with keen eyes. It was a well-appointed space —floral wallpaper, lace curtains, and a delicate four-poster bed covered in an embroidered counterpane. Lady Eleanor's jewelry box sat innocently upon her vanity, and the wardrobe doors stood ajar.

"Was the window open at any time from the moment you last saw the necklace until Lady Eleanor discovered it was gone?" the duke asked sharply, stepping toward it.

Martha shook her head. "No, your Grace. Lady Eleanor never opens it during the colder months. It was locked, just as it is now."

The duke's fingers tested the latch, and he nodded. "No sign of tampering. Whoever stole the necklace did not come in this way."

"Which leaves the door," I said.

Martha's expression grew troubled. "Lady Eleanor doesn't lock her door during the day. Only at nighttime."

"No forced entry, then," the duke said quietly. "The thief could have come in as easily as opening the door."

"Who knew that the necklace was in this room last night?" I asked Martha, my voice gentle.

"Miss Lavinia and Miss Felicity. They saw it when they arrived." Her eyes darted nervously toward the door as if the thief might be listening even now.

The duke turned to me with a wrinkle in his brow. "The cousins. Are they close to their brothers?"

"They are."

"That means we cannot rule out the possibility that the

men knew about it as well." He turned to Martha, "I need to ask you a few questions. Does Lady Eleanor have a sitting room?"

"Yes, Your Grace."

We followed her to the graciously appointed room which consisted of a seating arrangement, a desk, and several small tables. Just as we entered, the small carriage clock on the mantle over the fireplace chimed the two o'clock hour.

"Please take a seat, Martha," I said, taking the lead. The poor thing was pale as could be.

"Thank you, milady," she said, barely perching on the edge of the chair she chose.

The duke and I had previously decided I would interrogate the female staff and Eleanor's female cousins. He would question the men. So I led off with the statement that was the most natural. "As you know we're investigating the missing necklace."

"Yes, milady." Terror was evident in her eyes.

"You brought it to Lady Eleanor's room yesterday, correct?"

She nodded. "Just as my lady asked."

"Did you tell anyone that you had done so?" I pressed.

"No, I swear it," Martha said earnestly, her hands clenched tightly on her lap. "I didn't breathe a word of it to anyone. I only brought it to Lady Eleanor."

"What happened after you delivered it? Please be as specific as you can."

She seemed to relax a little as she searched her memory. "Lady Eleanor wanted to check the necklace to make sure the clasp was secure, which she did. And then she wanted to see how it looked with her ball gown. Just as I had placed it around her neck, her cousins arrived."

"Miss Lavinia and Miss Felicity?"

"Yes."

I believed her. Her sincerity was undeniable, and I could see the fear in her eyes—the kind that comes from someone who knows she's innocent yet fears she may not be believed. But I couldn't afford to trust instincts alone. "Did the cousins say anything about the necklace?"

"Oh, yes, milady. They oohed and aahed about it. When they said they wanted to hold it in their hands, Lady Eleanor asked me to unclasp it and give it to them. After a few minutes, milady asked me to put it back in the jewelry box."

"Did Miss Lavinia and Miss Felicity see the box?"

"Oh, yes. They couldn't have missed it."

"Did you return the box to its usual place?"

"Yes, Miss. In Lady Eleanor's vanity."

"Did they see you put it there?"

"My back was turned to them, so I couldn't say."

"But they could see you from where they were standing."

She breathed an easy sigh. She must have figured out where I was headed with my questions. In a firmer voice, she said, "Yes, milady. They could."

"You're doing very well, Martha. Now if we could move on to other questions. Is there any chance someone saw you deliver the necklace?" I asked. "Did you encounter anyone on the way?"

Martha's brow furrowed, and she shook her head slowly. "No, my lady. The hallways were quiet. I took care to be discreet."

The duke, who had been watching the exchange in silence, spoke up. "Where was the rest of the staff?"

"Well, it was time for our tea, Your Grace, so they were in the staff dining room, close to the kitchen."

"All of them?" the duke asked.

"I believe so."

"But you couldn't swear to it."

"No, Your Grace. After I stored the jewelry box in Lady

Eleanor's vanity, milady released me so I could have my tea as well. I was very excited about the ball. That was all everyone could talk about."

"Who was there?"

"Well, Cook, of course, the housekeeper, the butler." She continued to enumerate all the people who'd been in the staff dining room. While she did so, I jotted down the names on the notebook I always carry with me which I use to write my thoughts. In this instance, it would provide a record of everything surrounding this investigation.

"Is that it?" Steele asked when she was finished.

"Yes, Your Grace."

"You've done a fine job, Martha," I said. "Thank you. That will be all."

"Ta, milady." She curtsied again before leaving us.

I turned to the duke once she was gone. "She's telling the truth."

"She may be," he replied, his expression unreadable.

The rest of the afternoon passed in a blur of interviews. While I spoke to the female servants in the housekeeper's room, Steele questioned the men in the butler's pantry.

I faced an array of anxious maids, laundry women, kitchen staff, and everything in between. They all had stories —some conflicting, some vague, and some suspiciously rehearsed. But it all added up to the same conclusion. All of them had been too busy with their chores to wander into Eleanor's room and steal the necklace. And if they had, their absence would have been noted.

By the time I was finished, my head was spinning. It was a relief to finally step out of the stuffy room and breathe the cooler evening air filtering through the hallways. I made my way to my room so I could write a report of what I'd heard before dressing for supper.

I couldn't very well claim yet another headache, so I spent

the time after the evening meal socializing with the other guests. The time seemed to crawl by. But finally, around eleven, Eleanor suggested we seek our beds as she had much planned for the next day.

When I finally met the duke in the study, I was drooping with fatigue. It was no wonder as I'd had an early start this morning, followed by a full day. After a brief discussion, the duke suggested I read the report I'd brought. I didn't get far before I was stumbling through it, slurring my words.

It didn't take long for the duke to stop me. "Lady Rosalynd?"

I turned bleary eyes to him. "Yes, Your Grace."

"You seem . . . exhausted." His voice seemed to accuse more than care.

So, of course, my temper got the better of me. "I've been up since dawn, Your Grace. I arrived at Needham Hall looking forward to days of holiday merriment, only to become embroiled in an investigation. I now find myself consoling Eleanor, questioning staff, putting up with obnoxious cousins. And if all that were not enough, I'm now being censured by an overbearing duke."

That brow of his took a hike. "I haven't been dressed down that forcefully since my school days."

Heavens! What had I done? I'd insulted a duke! "I beg your pardon. I shouldn't have—"

"Found me overbearing?" His haughty tone was in full force. "Goes along with your titian tresses, I suppose. Redheads are famous for their fiery temperament."

Tempted as I was to retort in kind, I did not. Lashing out would not do. It would only prove his point. "I'm a very even-keeled person."

He sniffed. "All evidence to the contrary."

Was he trying to set me off again? What a horrid man!

"Well" —he shrugged— "as you are making no sense, let

us adjourn. We can reconvene in the morning after we've broken our fast. Say ten o'clock?"

I came to my feet and curtsied. "Of course, Your Grace. Good night."

He stretched out his arm toward me. "Leave your report. I'd like to read it before heading off to bed."

As I gave it to him, he bowed over my hand. Gazing into my eyes, he said in the smoothest tone I'd heard from him, "Good night, Lady Rosalynd. I wish you a restful sleep."

There would be little chance of that. My 'fiery' temperament would not allow it.

CHAPTER 5

THE SUSPECT LIST GROWS

I WOKE EARLIER than I intended, the winter sunlight barely filtering through the heavy damask curtains. Last night's discussion with Lady Rosalynd weighed on my conscience. I should not have baited her. She deserved better. I did not, however, wonder why I had acted in such a reprehensible manner.

I'd expected my stay at Needham Hall to consist of a serious discussion about Needham's proposed legislation and my attendance at the Christmas Ball, the latter a necessary evil I couldn't avoid in good grace. But it was turning out to be something rather more perilous. And it all came down to my unexpected attraction to Lady Rosalynd. The last time I'd felt the same about a lady, it had ended in tragedy. I simply could not, would not, give in to my impulses. I'd mastered them once. I could do so again.

At this point, my only responsibility lay in locating Lady Eleanor's missing necklace. Nothing else mattered. Once I'd done my duty, I would claim an urgent matter had come up at Steele Castle and leave.

Firmly in control of my emotions, I headed to the dining room, where breakfast was being served. I was not surprised to find the room empty. The family and guests were still abed. Once I'd had my fill, I proceeded to the study where Needham was waiting for me. The day before, we'd agreed to meet at nine so I could provide him with a summary of our progress. Although disappointed we weren't further along, he appreciated we had ruled out his household staff as suspects. Lady Rosalynd's report had reached the same conclusion I had.

"I suppose that only leaves my family and Cumberforth," he said in a lugubrious tone.

"It does look that way. But let us wait until we discover more facts before reaching that conclusion."

"Yes, of course. You're right." He somewhat brightened up. "Rosalynd should be of great help with that. She's quite a clever girl."

"I know." The report she'd written had been concise and complete. She'd concluded the female staff had been too busy with their chores to nip into Lady Eleanor's bedchamber and steal the necklace. Their absence would have been noted by others.

"It's a shame, really," Needham said.

"What is?"

"The mantle of responsibility she's taken on. Her brother, Earl Rosehaven, handles the finances, of course. But he leaves every other familial duty to Rosalynd. She's in charge of the upbringing of her sisters and younger brother—I believe there are six of them—as well as the management of Rosehaven Manor and their residence in London. At her age, she should be setting up her own nursery, not worrying about her brothers and sisters."

For the last five years, Needham had encouraged me to marry again. He'd argued that my wife's demise in childbirth, although tragic, did not mean it would happen again. I'd sidestepped the subject in the past, but now it seemed he was hinting at it once more. If that was the case, I could not let it pass. "If that is a veiled reference that I would make her a perfect husband—"

Needham laughed. "Oh, heavens no. I know how you feel about *that* particular subject." He waved a hand in the air. "And even if I were, it wouldn't do. The lady does not wish to marry. Imagine that! She would make an excellent wife given all the experience she's had. The family is quite prolific too. She has eight brothers and sisters."

"I thought you said six," I pointed out.

"Six younger, two older," Needham replied.

Before I could enquire why the lady did not wish to marry, Lady Rosalynd herself arrived. After greeting her, Needham excused himself and left us to it.

Going by her expression, she appeared peeved at me. Understandably so after what I'd said to her last night. Not my finest moment. I decided to offer an olive branch. "I read your report. Well written, complete. You don't think any female staff was involved."

She nodded. "They were either busy with their duties or enjoying their tea. Household staff, as I have cause to know, barely have a moment to themselves. If they had not adhered to their responsibilities, someone would have noticed. As I noted in my report, no one commented on such a thing."

"I concluded the same as far as the male staff. That leaves the cousins. And Cumberforth."

"Not Cumberforth."

"Why not?"

"He's in love with Eleanor."

"How do you know? As far as I know, he hasn't declared himself."

"I sat next to him yesterday during our luncheon. His eyes, his words, were all for Eleanor. He could hardly tear his gaze from her."

"Men's eyes and gazes can deceive." As I had good cause to know.

"Not Cumberforth. There's no guile in him."

"Even so, we will keep him on our list of suspects."

"You're wasting your time."

Amazing! She was arguing with me nce more. I pinned her with a hard gaze. "It's my time to waste, Lady Rosalynd."

She shrugged. "Yes, of course, Your Grace. I apologize."

She didn't appear the least bit sorry. But there was no time to dwell on it when we had a mystery to solve. "So? The cousins? How should we proceed?"

"We must speak to them today. There's no time to waste."

I nodded in agreement. Seemingly we had reached the same conclusion. Just as well. It would not help our mission if we were at odds with each other. "None of the cousins seem to have an inkling that the diamond necklace has gone missing."

"Yes, I rather think so. Except, of course, if one of them took it."

"We'll need to tread carefully with our questions."

"I agree."

Now that the ice between us had thawed, I took a seat on the sofa next to her. We discussed each cousin, weighing each one with a suspicious eye. Two gentlemen and two ladies, each with their own secrets and possible motives. After we'd thoroughly shared our opinions, we agreed to proceed as we'd done with the staff. I would speak with the male cousins, and she with the females. As time was not on our side—the Christmas Ball was a day away—we'd need to conduct our interviews this morning. Lady Eleanor's engagement announcement to Lord Cumberforth hung by a fraying thread.

"Will they speak freely, you think?" Lady Rosalynd asked, her brow furrowed.

"If we do our job well," I replied, "they won't even realize we're asking questions." She gave a nod, and we made our way out of the study, our plan firmly in place.

I'd decided to speak with the first cousin on my list—Alistair, Needham's heir and an avid sportsman. He tended not only to ride to hounds but also to wager on horse races and pugilistic endeavors. Whether he had the funds to do so was unknown to me. Something I would need to find out. I found him in the library, lounging with a cup of coffee and leafing through a newspaper that I knew had been delivered this morning.

"Good morning, Alistair," I said. Since all the cousins shared the same surname, during supper we'd agreed to greet them by their first one to avoid confusion.. "I trust you slept well?"

"Well enough, Steele," he replied with a lazy grin. "Eleanor certainly knows how to entertain."

"Indeed, she does," I agreed, taking a seat across from him. I steered the conversation toward generalities, speaking of London society, the latest gossip, and eventually—casually —of the costs of maintaining prime horseflesh.

Alistair, who was not shy about airing his opinions, spoke freely of the outrageous expenses he had incurred over the past year. A few minutes in, he was well into a tirade about the indignity of creditors. "It's a devil's game, I tell you," he complained, setting down his coffee with a thud. "Only last month, I was forced to part with my carriage. Imagine! A gentleman of my standing, reduced to hiring one like a commoner."

I murmured sympathetically, but my thoughts were racing. Alistair's betting debts were clearly a source of stress. Could desperation have driven him to theft?

I left him to his newspaper and sought out the second male cousin, Edwin. In many ways, the antithesis to his cousin, Edwin was an aspiring lawyer who brought a logical, somewhat skeptical approach to family matters. During yesterday's luncheon, he'd expressed a wish to set up his own practice in London. A venture his father approved of. While he did not appear to be overly social, like his cousin, he was attentive and observant, particularly when it came to matters involving the family fortune. Last night in the drawing room, he'd suggested a business scheme to his uncle that had proven lucrative to other investors. Needham had said he'd look into it.

I found Edwin in the drawing room seemingly immersed in reading a letter over a desk. As soon as I entered the room, he tucked the correspondence underneath the desk blotter which made me suspicious of what it contained.

"Good morning, Edwin," I said, once more feigning lightheartedness. "Lady Eleanor's household is certainly alive with the spirit of Christmas. The greenery is quite impressive."

"Yes, yes," he muttered, scarcely glancing up. "Eleanor does like to have things perfect."

I noted the strain in his voice. Curious. Last night he hadn't seemed to have a care in the world. Did the letter hold a clue to his change of mood? I would need to find out. As there was no time to waste, I tossed aside etiquette. "Anything wrong, old chap? You seem a tad upset?"

"Just got unsettling news."

"Oh?"

"Had my heart set on joining a law practice in London. But they hired someone with more experience."

"Tough luck, old man. There are others, though."

"Yes." He didn't appear too hopeful. "Thing is, funds are rather low. Needham paid my expenses at Oxford. But now I was hoping . . . well, you don't really want to hear my woes. I must learn to manage, even when there's not enough to go around." His bitterness was unmistakable which made me wonder if he had been tempted to solve his money troubles by pilfering Eleanor's diamonds.

Having finished with the two cousins, I headed back to Needham's study. On the way, I saw Lady Rosalynd finishing her conversation with Felicity, who appeared flustered and agitated. Going by Lady Rosalynd's expression, the conversation had been an enlightening one.

We exchanged but a brief glance, agreeing without words to head toward Needham's study. But before either of us could do so, our investigation was interrupted by the sound of horses and the crunch of carriage wheels on the gravel outside Needham Manor.

Almost on cue, Lady Eleanor drifted forward from a corridor, her arm curled around Lord Cumberforth's arm. "That must be Lord and Lady Burkett," she said as they rushed past us. Moments later, a footman confirmed her statement.

Rosalynd's eyes narrowed with barely concealed irritation. I didn't blame her. The arrival of the Burketts was a complication we did not need.

As Cumberforth's parents made their entrance, Lady Burkett caught sight of me. "Steele," she greeted me warmly, a bright smile lighting her face. "What a lovely surprise to see you here! Eleanor didn't mention you'd be visiting."

I offered a polite bow. "Dull fellow that I am, it must have slipped her mind."

Lady Burkett laughed. "Oh, come Steele. Last thing you

are is dull. Many a London hostess would give her eyeteeth for your presence at one of their balls."

"You flatter me, ma'am." I turned to my fellow sleuth. "Have you met Lady Rosalynd, Rosehaven's sister?"

"Can't say I've had the pleasure," Lady Burkett said. "How are you, my dear?"

"Fine, ma'am. Thank you for asking."

While Lady Burkett was a congenial and charming woman, her husband was just the opposite. Burkett was known far and wide for his dour demeanor and critical eye. His scowl deepened as he observed the festive decorations in the hall, his eyes flicking critically from the garlands to the servants bustling about. "A great deal of fuss," he muttered. "More than necessary, if you ask me."

Lady Burkett laughed, dismissing her husband's complaints with a wave of her hand. "Oh, you know Edward," she said to us with a conspiratorial smile. "Always the practical one."

I smiled tightly, making a mental note to keep a careful watch on the marquis. Something about his dour mood made me uneasy. He bore watching. Sooner or later, I would figure it out.

Without bothering to acknowledge Lady Rosalynd, Burkett addressed his son, "Stephen, I need a word."

"Of course, Father. Aren't you going to greet Lady Eleanor?"

My opinion of Cumberforth rose. He wasn't quite the milksop I thought he was. Maybe Rosalynd was right.

"Yes, of course. Lady Eleanor." Burkett barely nodded in her direction. Lady Burkett, on the other hand, exchanged cheek kisses with her. "You're so lovely Eleanor. Truly a rose in winter."

Lady Eleanor's cheeks pinked up, clearly pleased by the compliment. "Thank you, Lady Burkett."

Just then a gong sounded. "Oh, that's the signal for our luncheon," Lady Eleanor said. "It'll be served in twenty minutes."

"Well, that should give us plenty of time to refresh ourselves," Lady Burkett said with an uplift to her lips.

"And for me to talk to my son," Lord Burkett said.

Every gaze followed the Burketts and their son as they climbed the stairs to the first floor, Eleanor's the most worried of all.

Catching Rosalynd's attention, I nodded in the general direction of the study. A few minutes later, after taking different routes, we reached that destination. Once the door was shut, I wasted no time.

"Well?" I asked, eager to hear what she had learned.

Rosalynd's eyes glimmered with a mixture of excitement and concern. "I suspect Lavinia is in love with Lord Cumberforth," she revealed, her voice barely above a whisper. "She didn't say so directly, of course, but it's clear from the way she speaks of him. She became quite flustered when I mentioned his name."

"Interesting," I said, considering the implications. "And the other cousin? Felicity?"

"She detests him," Rosalynd said bluntly. "I'm certain of it. She was almost gleeful when she hinted at his faults and shortcomings, whether real or imagined. I suspect she would be delighted if his engagement to Eleanor was called off."

The pieces were beginning to form a picture, but it was not yet clear what the whole would be.

"What about you? What did you discover?" she asked, turning the conversation back to me.

I relayed my observations about the two male cousins—Alistair's gambling and Edwin's financial woes. Rosalynd's expression grew more troubled with every word, her fingers tapping restlessly on the arm of her chair.

"Any one of them could have taken the necklace."

"Or maybe more than one. They could have worked in tandem. There's no help for it," I said grimly. "We'll have to search their rooms."

Rosalynd hesitated, biting her lower lip as she considered the suggestion. It was a bold step and one that carried considerable risk. But we were running out of time, and if we didn't find some clue—some shred of evidence—Lady Eleanor's future would be in jeopardy.

The gong sounded again, the final signal to proceed to the dining room.

"How are we to achieve this?"

"Eleanor has something planned for this afternoon. It should provide us with plenty of time to do what must be done."

CHAPTER 6

~~~

A CLUE IS DISCOVERED

*A*FTER LUNCHEON, Eleanor had planned a skating party at a nearby pond. One which sadly I would not be attending. Claiming weak ankles, I once again excused myself from the activity. Eleanor had not questioned me—she knew me well enough to recognize when I had a purpose that would not be gainsaid.

Lavinia, however, had no such restraint. "Heavens," she said with a smirk. "You do have quite a number of ailments, Lady Rosalynd."

I pulled my shawl closer, feigning a delicate constitution I did not possess. In reality, I had always enjoyed robust health and skating was a favorite pastime. I loved the way the winter air bit at my cheeks and the sense of freedom that came with gliding across the ice. But today was not a day for pleasure, not when Eleanor's future remained shrouded in uncertainty. "I shall rest by the fire and take tea," I said in my most convincing imitation of convalescence.

"Better you than me," Lavinia said, heading off.

The duke had begged off as well, providing the explanation he'd be discussing a proposed legislative measure with Lord Needham. No one questioned his choice.

Alas! Such was the way of the world. Most women's actions were thoroughly scrutinized and, in many instances, criticized. Men, on the other hand, could do all manners of evil, and no one censured their deeds.

Once the skating party went on their merry way, the great hall fell suddenly silent, the absence of voices and footsteps amplifying my awareness of the task ahead. It would not be long before the duke and I began our clandestine search.

Surprisingly, my heart fluttered with the thrill of it. It was as if I were a character in one of those sensational novels I pretended not to read, sneaking about in shadows and hunting for the truth. The fact I'd be performing this task alongside the duke did not factor into it. Or so I told myself.

Eager to start the search, I made my way to the library, where the duke awaited me. As before, he stood by the mantel, his expression calm but his eyes burning with determination.

"They've gone," I said, closing the door behind me. "We have at least two hours, perhaps three if they dawdle over the hot chocolate and refreshments that will be served."

"Then we mustn't waste a moment," he replied, his voice low and controlled. "You'll take the women's rooms, and I'll take the men's."

"As we agreed, yes."

He glanced at his pocket watch. "It's half past one. Let's meet back here at three. That should give us more than enough time to perform the search."

"We do want to be thorough."

He nodded toward the door. "You should leave first. I'll follow in ten minutes."

"Good luck," I said with a grin.

"*Bonne chance*," he replied tight lipped.

In the next instant, I made my way out of the study. Making sure I was not seen, I headed upstairs to the second floor where Felicity's and Lavinia's chambers were located. Every creak of the floorboards beneath my feet heightened my sense of urgency.

The first door I came to was Lavinia's. I hesitated for only a moment before opening it, stepping quietly inside, and closing the door behind me. Her chamber was elegant, a reflection of Eleanor's refined taste. There was nothing overtly out of place, but I knew better than to be deceived by the outward appearance of order. My eyes scanned the room swiftly, noting the small writing desk in the corner, the neat vanity table, and the sumptuous bed draped with an embroidered coverlet.

Since I knew Lavinia was a frequent correspondent, I went to the writing desk first. Her letters from her London friends were numerous and filled with carefully penned lines about fashion, balls, eligible gentlemen, and town rumors. I leafed through the stack quickly, my fingers moving with practiced efficiency. There were invitations to parties, receipts from dressmakers, and a half-finished letter to a close friend detailing the latest gossip about Eleanor and Lord Cumberforth. I could almost feel Lavinia's jealousy oozing from the words.

But I found nothing that suggested theft or blackmail. Closing the desk drawer with a soft sigh, I moved on to the wardrobe. Inside, I found rows of beautifully tailored gowns, shawls, and fur-lined cloaks, but nothing out of the ordinary. My frustration was beginning to mount. Given Lavinia's penchant for gossip, I'd hoped to find something more concrete.

The fear that I was wasting precious time weighed heavily on me. I was about to leave when my gaze fell upon a small jewelry box on the bedside table. My heart leapt. I hadn't noticed it before, tucked away as it was behind a pile of novels.

My pulse quickening, I opened it carefully. Inside were delicate pearls, a sapphire ring, and a small diamond brooch —family pieces, no doubt, but no sign of Eleanor's missing necklace. I closed the lid and stood back, feeling the familiar stirrings of disappointment. Lavinia's room, as far as I could tell, held no clues.

With a renewed sense of urgency, I left her chamber and made my way down the hall to Felicity's. The contrast between the two women's rooms was striking. Felicity's was less meticulous, with papers and books strewn about her desk and the faint scent of lavender in the air. I began my search with the desk, picking through correspondence that ranged from mundane to outright vicious.

One letter in particular caught my eye. It was addressed to a confidante in London. Felicity had written with undisguised glee about her disdain for Lord Cumberforth. She described him as "arrogant, dull-witted, and utterly undeserving of any woman's affection."

The sentiment surprised me. Cumberforth was neither arrogant nor dull-witted. And the claim he was undeserving of a woman's affection was utterly nonsensical. One only had to witness his interactions with Eleanor to understand he was everything a young gentleman in love should be.

But then that was the crux of the matter, wasn't it? Cumberforth had totally ignored Felicity, something she bitterly resented. Could that disdain have driven her to sabotage Eleanor's engagement by stealing the necklace? It certainly made for a good theory. But without proof, it was just that. I needed to find something to prove she was the culprit.

Turning to the wardrobe, I rummaged through shawls, coats, and half-forgotten hats. Then I noticed something—one of the hatboxes was unusually heavy. With trembling fingers, I opened it, half-expecting to see the necklace glinting at me from within. But it was empty save for an old velvet pouch containing an assortment of tarnished silver hairpins. Frustrated, I set it aside and continued my search.

It was then that I spotted a crumpled piece of paper wedged between the wardrobe and the wall. It looked as if it had been stuffed there in haste, barely visible behind the folds of a dark green cloak. I pulled it out, my heart beating faster as I smoothed the paper on my knee.

It was a torn letter, the edges ragged, and the ink smeared. The handwriting was unfamiliar, the script jagged as if written in a great rush. The words, however, were unmistakable:

"You have done a great wrong. You must put things right, or I will reveal all. I have no wish to cause a scandal, but you leave me no choice. Do not think that I will hesitate to act."

There was no signature. My mind reeled as I reread the letter, my thoughts racing with possibilities. Was Felicity being blackmailed over a perceived wrongful action? She was the likely recipient as the note was found in her wardrobe. But who had written it? And had it really been addressed to her? Felicity's room offered no further answers, but the letter was evidence.

I slipped the letter into a hidden pocket in my gown, my pulse racing with a new sense of purpose. The necklace might not have been found, but this clue was more valuable than gold. With renewed determination, I hurried back to the library, eager to compare my findings with the duke.

He was already there when I entered, pacing before the fireplace with a stormy expression. No wonder. I was twenty minutes past our agreed-upon time. "I apologize for keeping you waiting. The search took longer than I expected. But I did want to be thorough."

He brushed a hand across his brow. "No need to apologize. I feared you'd been caught."

I spread my arms wide. "As you see, I wasn't. And even if I had, I would have offered a simple explanation for my being in the lady's room. A pair of gloves left behind, a perfume I wished to borrow. No servant would have questioned me."

"The maid might have reported your intrusion to her mistress."

"Eleanor's cousins never bring their own servants. They depend on Eleanor's staff to handle their needs. So any report would have been given to Eleanor. She would have thanked the maid and told her there was nothing to worry about."

His brow wrinkled. "You're very well informed."

"Eleanor is my best friend. We've been visiting each other's homes for more than a dozen years. I'm very familiar with how Needham Hall is run. But enough of that." Flashing a triumphant grin, I asked, "Would you like to hear what I found?"

"The necklace?"

I shook my head. "Sadly, no. But something almost as good. I found a letter. It speaks of a wrong committed and a threat to reveal all, whatever that might be."

After I handed the note to him, his brow furrowed deeper with every line he read. "Do you think it was addressed to Felicity?" he asked.

"Could be. But the letter isn't signed, and I have no idea who wrote it—or to whom it was written. She could have been planning to send it."

"Or she could be its recipient," the duke said in a somber tone.

"The great wrong must be the theft of the necklace, don't you think?" I asked.

"Maybe. Or maybe something else we have yet to determine. In either case, someone in this house is being blackmailed," he said finally, looking up at me with an intensity that made my breath catch. "Whoever it is may have been desperate enough to steal the necklace."

"For what reason?" I asked, as a chill ran down my spine.

"That we must find out," he said, his voice resolute. He tucked the letter inside his coat as his determined gaze met mine. "We'll need to keep this to ourselves for now, until we know more. If the parties involved discover we've found a clue, they may take more drastic steps."

I nodded as a thrill of excitement mingled with my apprehension. "We will find out who is behind this," I said, my voice firm with conviction.

The duke's lips twitched in a hint of a smile. Why, that totally transformed his whole face. He no longer seemed aloof, arrogant. Although miles away from affable, he seemed more... approachable.

"I have no doubt we will," he said. "But we must tread carefully from here on. The closer we get, the more dangerous this investigation will become."

He was right, of course. We were walking a narrow path. One wrong step could spell disaster. But first things first. "We'll need to determine whose hand wrote that blackmail note."

He nodded. "I have an idea."

CHAPTER 7

CHRISTMAS WISHES

THE EVENING BUZZED with the pleasant hum of conversation as the guests of Needham Hall gathered in the grand drawing room after supper. The skating party had left everyone rosy-cheeked and in high spirits. Not only that but new guests had arrived, including Lord Hungerford, a friend of Alistair from his Oxford days. With the addition of the new guests, the room crackled with anticipation as I prepared to unveil this evening's diversion.

But first, Lady Eleanor had to explain what was about to happen. She clapped to get everyone's attention. As the room quieted down, she said with a smile. "The Duke of Steele has been gracious enough to plan a game for us. I hope you will all participate." Turning to me, she said, "If you will, Your Grace."

Standing near the hearth, I cast a glance over the assembled crowd. Lady Eleanor glowed with happiness, laughing softly as she settled next to Cumberforth. Rosalynd observed the gathering with her usual air of composed curiosity. Her sharp gaze, I knew by now, missed very little—a quality I had come to value in our recent efforts.

Drawing myself up, I cut through the hum of chatter. "Ladies and gentlemen," I announced, "I have devised a little game for us this evening—a game of wit, creativity, and perhaps, a touch of mischief."

The guests murmured in interest, leaning forward in their chairs.

"Each of you," I continued, gesturing toward the crystal bowl on the side table, "will write a Christmas wish. Not an ordinary wish, mind you, but something outrageous, imaginative—perhaps even scandalous. You'll sign your name, fold the card, and place it in the bowl. I shall read each wish aloud, and we'll try to guess the author. The one who guesses correctly most often will win."

"And what will this grand prize be, Your Grace?" Lady Eleanor asked, her cheeks flushed with the warmth of the fire and good cheer.

I allowed a smile to spread across my face. "Eternal glory, naturally. And this splendid box of chocolate truffles, direct from Belgium." I held up the gift I'd intended to present to Lady Eleanor as a thank you for being included in her Christmas Ball festivities. Before supper, I'd revealed the game and asked for her permission to use it as a prize.

The room erupted in laughter and applause.

Moving toward the stack of cards and pens, I distributed the materials, pausing briefly beside Rosalynd. "What shall your outrageous wish be, Lady Rosalynd?" I asked quietly, my voice low enough for her ears alone.

Her lips curved into the faintest smile. "That, Your Grace, would spoil the game."

I watched in silence as she selected a card with deliberate grace. Her composure was unshakable, but I could sense the sharpness of her mind at work. Tonight's game was a charming distraction for the guests, but for Rosalynd and me, it was a means to an end. Somewhere in this room, the person who had written the blackmail note was watching, unaware they were under suspicion.

Once all the wishes were written and placed in the bowl, I took center stage. Drawing the first card with theatrical flair, I read aloud: *I wish to own a castle in every country, each staffed with a fleet of butlers who speak only in limericks.*

The room exploded with laughter.

"Who among you harbors such whimsical ambitions?" I demanded, my tone mock-serious as I surveyed the room.

"Lady Eleanor!" Cumberforth exclaimed, nodding toward his fiancée, whose complexion turned a charming shade of pink. "She is a dab hand at managing Needham Hall."

"Not guilty!" she protested.

With a rueful grin, Lavinia raised her hand. "The butlers were my idea. I confess."

The game continued, each wish drawing peals of laughter or playful accusations. I played my part well, keeping the mood light. But my mind never strayed far from my true purpose. I kept an eye on each guest's reactions, noting who seemed overly amused, too guarded, or suspiciously disengaged.

Finally, after the last wish was read and the truffles triumphantly claimed by Lady Eleanor who generously offered to share them with her guests, I turned toward Lady Rosalynd, my tone dropping to a confidential murmur. "Shall we adjourn to the study?"

She nodded, her expression serene, though her eyes held the glint of determination. Laying claim to exhaustion, she wandered out of the drawing room.

As for myself, Needham asked me to join him in the study for a nightcap. Not unexpectedly, I'd previously informed him of our plans and devised this stratagem. We arrived at his study to find a servant had already delivered the crystal bowl full of wishes. Just as he was pouring generous splashes of brandy into two glasses, Rosalynd entered the room. After a brief discussion about the state of the investigation, Needham left us to it.

The study was quieter than the lively drawing room, its atmosphere subdued by the weight of our task. Without being prompted, Rosalynd carefully unfolded the blackmail note we had examined earlier in the day, smoothing the creased paper with steady hands.

"The handwriting," she said, placing the note beside the stack of discarded wish cards. "It's bold, hurried. Almost reckless."

I leaned over the desk, my eyes sharply scanning the note. "A person under duress, perhaps," I mused. "Or someone unaccustomed to such deceptions. Let us see if our game has revealed anything useful."

One by one, we compared the cards to the blackmail note. Rosalynd's eye for detail was unmatched, and I marveled at the precision with which she examined each flourish and stroke.

"What do you think of this one?" I asked, passing her a card that read: *I wish for a Christmas pudding so large it could feed all of London.*

"Lady Eleanor's," she said. "She has the kindest heart of all."

I nodded, as she set the card aside. We worked through the pile systematically, discarding possibilities as the room grew quieter, the tension mounting with each eliminated suspect.

At last, only one card remained. Rosalynd's eyes narrowed as she compared the bold, erratic handwriting to the note.

"This is it," she said softly, her voice tinged with both triumph and unease.

I took the card and read aloud: *I wish to own a castle in every country, each staffed with a fleet of butlers who speak only in limericks.*

"Lavinia," Lady Rosalynd said grimly. "She claimed it as hers during the game. She must have seen Felicity take the necklace. It's the only explanation that makes any sense. She's threatening to reveal all unless Felicity returns it." She paused for a moment. "She also hinted at a scandal."

"Wouldn't the theft of the necklace suffice as one?"

Rosalynd shook her head. "I don't think so. Felicity could simply say she borrowed it because she wanted to see it up close. The family would smooth over the entire thing." She glanced up at me. "No. It's more than that. But what could it be? I know of no scandal that pertains to Felicity."

"There's only one way to find out," I said. We'll need to confront Lavinia. But we'll need to take care. She might perceive our intrusion as a threat, and desperation can drive even the most respectable person to extremes." As I had good cause to know. I'd once made that fatal mistake and been paying for it ever since. A familiar darkness descended upon me as it often did when I thought of that time.

Unaware of my mood shift, Rosalynd said, "Not tonight, though. We must gather more evidence before we act. The Needhams deserve better than a scandal on their doorstep."

Almost absentmindedly, I brushed a hand across my brow. "Yes. We must avoid that at all costs."

She glanced toward the door. "I'll leave first, shall I?" The same words she used before.

As I did. "Be careful you're not seen." And then I spoke without thinking. "It wouldn't do to set off a scandal."

She gazed at me, a confused look in her eyes. "What do you mean?"

"Lady Rosalynd and the Duke of Steele alone in Lord Needham's study," I explained. "There's no telling what they might have been up to in the dark."

For a moment, she appeared stunned. "Why would anybody think anything of the sort?"

"They overheard Needham and I discuss a meeting in the study."

"He's not here!"

"But you and I are. And that makes it so much worse. It wouldn't take more than that for a rumormonger like Lavinia to invent a lurid tale. You did say her correspondence was full of gossip, didn't you?"

She shook her head, causing a glorious disarray of her copper curls. "It won't wash, Steele.

"Why not?"

"Well, for one, I'm not in the market for a husband. And you don't intend to marry again."

How the devil did she know that? Aside from my family and Needham, I hadn't made that intention known. I took several steps toward her until we were standing a mere foot apart. A fiery tress had fallen across her face. Giving in to temptation, I tucked it behind her ear. "How very innocent you are," I whispered in a husky tone.

She bristled at that. "I'm not—well, I am—but that doesn't mean—"

I placed a finger on her mouth to shush her, to feel the softness of her lips. "A man and a woman don't have to intend marriage to make love."

She drew herself up to her full height which wasn't much. She only came up to my chin. "I know. I'm not that naive," she said, clearly offended. "But that's not something I would ever do."

The devil in me made me lean forward and murmur in her ear. "Even when you're attracted to a man?"

She stiffened but held her stand. "You think I'm attracted to you?"

"Oh, my dear, I know you are."

She hitched up her chin. "I'm not your dear, and you, sir, are no gentleman."

Brushing my thumb across her heated cheek, I whispered. "I never said I was."

She shot me a furious glance, turned, and stormed out.

Quietly closing the door behind her, I stood for a moment breathing in her lingering scent. A concoction of Lily of the Valley and her own bewitching brew. In desperate need of a drink, I poured a healthy splash of brandy into my glass and drank it down in one gulp. That had been rather bad of me. But somehow I couldn't find the will to regret it.

CHAPTER 8

A REVELATORY CONVERSATION

I AWAKENED BLEARY-EYED. No wonder. I'd tossed and turned half the night, my thoughts reliving what happened in Needham's study. After last night's debacle, my first inclination was to have Tilly pack my trunk and leave. But I'd never been a coward. I wasn't about to start now.

How dare the high and mighty Duke of Steele attempt to seduce me? And in Lord Needham's study of all places. Not that there was a proper place to do such a thing. He'd brushed up against me. Well, nearly. He had touched me, though. He'd been so close I'd breathed in that maddening scent of his. What was it? Sandalwood, cedar, some woodsy cologne? And underneath it all, him.

Plain and simple, I'd been mesmerized. No man had ever affected me the way he had. But I was not the least bit interested in a seduction, or a liaison, never mind marriage. I was way too busy with the upbringing of my siblings. And I couldn't very well leave them to Cosmos's mercies. Oh, he would feed and water them, put a roof over their heads, educate them. But he would never encourage their dreams or soothe their fears, most especially Petunia's. No. I could not leave my brothers and sisters to his care.

For years, I'd told myself I had no desire to marry. Not with all the responsibilities I had. My family being the most important. But there was also the Society for the Advancement of Women. We were planning big things, and I'd been elected its president. Come the season, we intended to submit a petition for woman suffrage to Parliament. A marriage, with all its responsibilities, would mean I would need to resign that office. With no firm hand to guide them, the Society would descend into chaos.

My well-ordered life had a purpose. Several of them in fact. I was . . . content. But then the Duke of Steele had breezed into my life, and we'd joined forces to find Eleanor's missing necklace. Our investigation had proceeded apace. We'd interviewed suspects and discovered clues. We'd analyzed everything and were moving in a forward path. I'd been content, excited over the investigation. Until last night when the duke tried to seduce me.

"He didn't seduce you," my conscience argued.

"He came damn close," I argued back.

"It takes two, Rosalynd. All you had to do was leave."

"Which I did," I rightfully pointed out.

"Well, there you go."

Honestly, sometimes my conscience was downright unbearable. But maybe 'she' was right. He hadn't seduced me. At the very least, a seduction involved kissing. Did it not? And he hadn't done that. But he'd tucked a lock of my hair behind my ear, laid a finger across my lips, whispered in my ear. His actions had been so unexpected I'd frozen in place. Why had he done such things? If it wasn't a seduction, what was it? Was he teasing? No. He was not that kind of man. Was he trying to irk me? Well, he'd succeeded at that. But again, the question was why?

A knock on the door interrupted my argument with myself.

"Milady?" Tilly, my maid.

"Come," I yelled.

"I brought your tea."

"Thank you, Tilly. Please put it on the table."

Once she'd done so, she asked, "Would you like me to draw your bath?"

"Yes, please." There was no more time to worry about the duke. I needed to ready myself for the day ahead.

Bathed and dressed, I headed toward the dining room where breakfast awaited the early risers.

But on my way, a faint murmur of voices from a side room reached my ears. Pausing just outside the half-open door, I recognized the unmistakable tones of Felicity and her brother Edwin. Pausing, I strained to make out their conversation.

"You shouldn't have done what you did, Felicity," Edwin's clear masculine voice said.

"Why should Cumberforth enjoy a life of luxury while you're left begging for crumbs?"

"Because he's Burkett's heir. He's entitled to it all. Can't you see that?"

"It should all have been yours."

"That's not the way the laws of primogeniture work. They're set in stone."

"Stop being such a milksop, Edwin."

"I'm not," he sounded affronted. "I'm only thinking of what's right."

"You're owed your share of the Burkett fortune. I'll make sure you get it."

"How will you manage that?"

"Lord Burkett promised to provide you with the inheritance you're due and settle a dowry on me."

"In exchange for what?"

"Eleanor's necklace. When she appears at the ball without it, he'll refuse to acknowledge her engagement to his son."

"Where will he get the money? It's common knowledge he's squandered the Burkett fortune on bad investments and excessive gambling."

"He intends for Cumberforth to marry Lady Annabel Bingham."

"He would never do that. He loves Eleanor. You've sold your honor to a man who will give you nothing in return."

"You're wrong. The Burketts have money. How else would they afford their luxurious lifestyle?"

"It's all for show, Felicity. There's no fortune behind the facade." Edwin temporarily paused. "Your actions will brand me a bastard and bring shame to our family."

"You'll have plenty of money to compensate for your disgrace."

"I'd rather be seen as Papa's legitimate son than Burkett's bastard."

"Even if you're poor as a church mouse?"

"Yes, even so."

"Well, I'm not willing to live a life of penury. A generous dowry means I can marry a peer, lead a comfortable life."

"Lavinia will expose you. She will brand you a thief. No peer will marry you."

"She can't prove it. I made sure I wasn't seen."

"I beg you to return the necklace, Felicity."

"Too late. I've already given it to Lord Burkett. He will provide us with a draft for twenty thousand pounds tonight. Half of it will be yours."

"I don't want any part of it. I'm leaving."

I rushed to step back from the door, my slippered feet moving silently on the thick carpet as I hid from view behind one of the many Christmas trees that had been placed around the hall. Felicity quickly followed her brother out of the side room. But rather than follow him up the stairs, she paused. Her brow wrinkled as she gazed around, probably to make sure no one had overheard their conversation. Little did she know she was much too late. A few moments later, she shrugged and moved in the direction of the dining room.

As I had suspected, Felicity had stolen the necklace, and she'd already passed it to Lord Burkett. Edwin's connection to Lord Cumberforth's family was unexpected. Lavinia somehow believed that Edwin had been born on the wrong side of the blanket, and Lord Burkett was his father.

The grandfather clock in the hall chimed the hour—eight o'clock. There was no time to waste. I had to let the duke know right away what I'd learned. The recollection of last night rose unbidden in my mind. We hadn't exactly parted amicably. Just the opposite. I'd stormed out of the study. But my feelings were not important. Finding Eleanor's necklace was. Last night be damned.

I carefully made my way to the duke's bedchamber making sure I wasn't seen. If someone caught me slipping into his room, my reputation would be ruined. Thankfully, none of the other guests seemed to be awake. Once I reached the duke's chamber, I knocked softly on the wood panel. A gentleman dressed in a servant's garment answered the door.

"I'm Lady Rosalynd. I need to speak to His Grace. It's a matter of some urgency," I announced in a whisper.

"Roberts? What is it?" the duke's voice demanded.

"Lady Rosalynd, Your Grace."

He appeared barely half-dressed. Trousers donned, thank heaven, but his shirt was half open, revealing more than was proper. "What are you doing here?"

I pushed my way past his valet. "We must talk. I overheard a conversation."

The duke turned to his manservant. "Roberts, that will be all." His dark hair gleamed wet, evidence he'd just bathed.

"Your Grace." His valet bowed before making his way out of the chamber, the door closing softly behind him.

Steele's angry gaze landed on me. "If anybody saw you, a scandal will most surely ensue." And then without the slightest thought to etiquette, he proceeded to button his shirt to his neck. He could have at least excused himself to finish dressing.

"I made sure I wasn't."

He propped his hands on his hips. "You've discovered something?"

I crossed the room to be closer to him. I wanted to make sure no one overheard us. Or so I told myself. "I overheard a conversation between Felicity and her brother, Edwin," I said without preamble. "She stole the necklace for Lord Burkett. He promised her a dowry and generous funds for her brother." I paused to get a breath. "But that's not all. Edwin is Burkett's illegitimate son."

For the next few minutes, he proceeded to drill me about the details. How did I know it had been Felicity and Edwin? Where were they? How close was I to the door?

He was insufferable. Did he think I'd made it all up? "I heard what I heard, Steele. There's no fault in my hearing or my sight."

"No need to get into a snit. I believed your first telling."

"Then why did you interrogate me?"

"You'll need to repeat word for word what you just told me to Lord Needham. I wanted to make sure you were letter perfect before you do."

"Oh!" I felt a fool. "Do you really think Edwin is Burkett's illegitimate son?"

"That will need to be determined. Not by me, nor you. Needham and his youngest brother will need to hash that out. I believe he's expected today." He moved into a room connected to the one we occupied, emerging moments later fully dressed. A vest and a coat now completed his ensemble. Except for his Snow White shirt, everything else was black.

"I'll go first," he said. "If the coast is clear, I'll crack open the door so you can emerge."

"Thank you."

"No need to thank me, Lady Rosalynd. I don't wish to embroil myself in a scandal any more than you do." He'd once more assumed his tight lipped expression. "The only way out of that would be a wedding. And neither of us wish for that debacle."

Just like that, we were back to where we'd been last night. At odds with each other. My stay at Needham Hall could not end fast enough. "No indeed, Your Grace."

With a nod, he slipped out the door. A few moments later, the door snicked open. Glancing right and left, I made my way from the room. Thankfully, no one was in sight. At the top of the stairs, I greeted the duke with a simple "Good morning." If anyone was within earshot, they would not remark upon it.

Silently, we made our way to the dining room where we found several guests enjoying their breakfast. Because the ball would be held tonight, there were no festivities planned this morning. We were meant to rest and enjoy ourselves before the evening ball.

As we approached the baseboard where the dishes had been laid out, the duke dropped a soft word in Lord Needham's ear who simply nodded. Eleanor wore an air of anxiety about her. Cumberforth sat next to her quietly conversing with her. Neither Felicity nor Edwin was present. But Lord and Lady Burkett as well as Lavinia and her brother, Alastair, were. He didn't appear to have a care in the world. Lavinia's face, however, was a mirror image of Eleanor's. I couldn't believe she'd carry through with her threat. But then she had her own objectives. Did she hope by revealing all, the engagement would end? If she thought such a thing, she was a fool. Eleanor and Cumberforth were deeply in love with each other. I only hoped that everything would be cleared by tonight.

CHAPTER 9

THE SECRETS IN THE SHADOWS

*A*FTER BREAKFAST, Lady Rosalynd and I proceeded to Needham's study to discuss what she'd learned. It took no time to share that information with our host. To say he was troubled was an understatement. So much so, he took pacing before me, his features tight with worry. Only to be expected after what Lady Rosalynd had revealed.

"We must retrieve Eleanor's necklace without causing a scandal. What are we to do?" His voice held a note of desperation.

I did not immediately answer Needham's plea but allowed the silence to settle before I spoke. "The situation is precarious. If Lord Burkett exposes Lady Eleanor's lack of dowry—thanks to Felicity's betrayal—the engagement will collapse. Worse still, if Lavinia reveals Edwin is Lord Burkett's illegitimate son, the Needham name could be destroyed entirely."

"I can't believe Edwin's mother would have played my brother false."

"If I may, Lord Needham" —Rosalynd interjected— "we don't actually have proof of that. Could it be conjecture on Felicity's part?"

"Edwin was born rather early into their marriage, seven months to be exact. And Burkett has been one of her suitors. But my brother Martin never once doubted Edwin was his son."

"Maybe he did not know. Maybe the lady dallied with Lord Burkett before their marriage."

Lord Needham's brow took a hike. "Charlotte, dally? She was a timid, quiet mouse who barely spoke in social gatherings, even family ones. No. She couldn't have been involved in a dalliance."

"And yet, Edwin was born early."

"He was rather small. Everyone wondered how he survived. His mother, sadly, did not." Needham glanced at me. "Much like your own wife—"

I froze as the pain of that memory stabbed at me cutting off my breath.

"I beg your pardon. That was an unforgivable thing to say. I need a drink, and so do you." Needham approached the cupboard, poured whiskey into two glasses, and handed one to me. Without a word, I gulped down the fiery liquor.

Too late recalling the other person in the room, Needham turned to her. "Lady Rosalynd?"

"None for me, thank you."

"Of course, my dear." Needham sipped at his while an awkward silence filled the room.

But it didn't last long. Lady Rosalynd soon stepped into the void. "Eleanor said your brother Martin will be attending the ball."

Needham cleared his throat. "Yes, he should be arriving

soon. His business interests in London kept him from arriving before today."

"Forgive me if I'm stepping out of line, Lord Needham. I treasure my brothers and sisters and would do anything for them. But Felicity does not seem to care that her actions would precipitate a scandal that would destroy not only your family's reputation but her brother, most particularly. And I have to wonder why that is."

"My brother Martin married twice. His first wife was Felicity's mother. We cautioned him against doing so. She was too young and too eager to enjoy what life had to offer to settle into the role of a proper wife. Sadly, my words proved to be true. A year after Felicity's birth, she deserted him. Martin searched for her, of course, only to discover she'd run away with a sugar plantation owner. Their ship capsized on the way to Jamaica. All souls aboard were lost at sea. Her body was never found so Martin had to wait seven years for her to be declared dead. As soon as she was, he married Charlotte. Seven months after that, Edwin was born. You know the rest."

Eager to move the conversation away from a topic that struck too close to home, I said, "I understand Edwin has the ambition of becoming a solicitor.".

"Yes, he attended Oxford and got a first in jurisprudence. His father encouraged him to learn a trade. He chose that field of study."

"A noble profession," I said.

"Unfortunately, he has not been able to make his way."

"Why not?"

"He's seen as a dilettante by those in that field. Untrue. He's quite serious in his pursuit."

"Once this matter is settled satisfactorily, I would be glad to put in a good word for him."

Needham's surprised gaze found me. "You'd do that?"

"He struck me as a serious young man, and he denounced his sister for her actions. I would need to have further discussions with him before I take that step, of course. But if I'm convinced he's everything I think he is, I would be glad to sponsor him."

"Thank you, Steele. That means the world to me."

"It's the least I can do. We would first need to solve our current conundrum, however. Otherwise, he'd have no future."

"I've been thinking," Rosalynd said. She sat across from me, poised, her hands folded as if carved from marble. But her eyes—those sharp, unyielding eyes—revealed the torrent of her thoughts.

"You've determined a course of action," I said. She'd come up with a plan while I'd been wallowing in despair.

"I have." She leaned forward, her voice steady but urgent. "If the necklace is in Lord Burkett's possession, we must reclaim it without alerting him."

Needham's knuckles whitened against the arms of his chair. "How? The man is shrewd. He'll never willingly part with it."

Rosalynd smiled faintly, it was the sort that held the promise of mischief. "Not willingly, no. But he needn't know it's gone until it's too late."

Intrigued by her words, I asked, "You propose a theft, Lady Rosalynd?"

"A reclamation," she corrected. "If Felicity had no qualms stealing from Eleanor, then we are justified in retrieving what's rightfully hers. But I would need assistance to access Burkett's quarters. He'll keep it close, I'm certain."

This was a bold woman, and I appreciated boldness. My lips curved in approval. "A daring plan. I like it."

"Highly irregular!" Needham sputtered, his expression torn between reluctance and desperation.

"Desperate times," I countered smoothly, "demand unconventional measures." I turned back to Rosalynd. "Lady Rosalynd, you and I will manage this. Burkett is unlikely to suspect a young lady, and I have some experience with subtle extractions."

She arched an elegant brow at me, her skepticism wrapped in charm. "Experience, Your Grace?"

"Let's say my education wasn't confined to the classics," I replied dryly, my tone making it clear I wasn't about to elaborate.

Needham sighed heavily. "Do what you must. But if Felicity discovers this, she may retaliate."

Rosalynd's expression darkened. "She must be removed from the field of play."

"You don't intend to harm her?" Needham exclaimed, his expression a study in horror.

Lady Rosalynd grinned. "No, Lord Needham. Only arrange for her to be somewhere else. She can't interfere with our plans or even learn about them if she's away from Needham Hall. I suggest you tell Eleanor what we've discovered. Have her take Felicity on a carriage ride with Cumberforth and Lord Harringford. She seemed quite taken with him last night."

"But where would they go?" He gazed out the window. "The weather has turned. We might even get some snow."

"Your local church. Harringford was waxing poetic about it last night. Something about its medieval spire. That should keep them far from here until this afternoon. By then, we shall have located the necklace."

"Good heavens, Rosalynd," Needham said. "I did not know you had such deviousness in you."

"Comes from having eight brothers and sisters, many of whom get up to all kinds of trouble." She turned to me and asked, "That plan should work, don't you think?"

"As long as Felicity agrees, I don't see why not."

"What about Lavinia?" Needham asked. "She needs to be dealt with as well."

"Her threat to expose Edwin's lineage requires a different strategy," Rosalynd said with conviction.

Meeting her gaze, I inclined my head. "Lady Rosalynd is correct. Lavinia must be incentivized to keep her silence."

Running a hand over his face, Needham sank into a chair. "What incentive could possibly work? The woman thrives on chaos."

"Her life's ambition is to marry a peer of the realm," Rosalynd said. "She can't very well do that if a particularly nasty rumor is spread about her. She loves gossip and knows how damaging it can be."

"What kind of rumor?" Needham asked.

"I'm sure Eleanor will come up with something."

"My Eleanor would never devise, much less spread, a nasty rumor!" Lord Needham exclaimed.

"Eleanor's entire future is on the line, Lord Needham. The mere threat of such a rumor would be enough to silence Lavinia, especially when confronted with her own misdeed. Talk to Eleanor. Once you explain what she must do, I believe she will gladly go along with the plan."

Needham threaded a hand through his hair. "How are we to get everything accomplished? The ball is tonight. Without the necklace, Burkett will call off his son's engagement."

"You're correct. We don't have a moment to waste," Lady Rosalynd said. "After you talk to Eleanor, ask Burkett for a moment of his time. Tell him you wish to discuss Eleanor's dowry."

"He doesn't think it's enough."

"Doesn't matter. Once he arrives, let us know. We'll be in the orangery."

"I suppose that's as good a place as any," I said.

Before we left, Needham said, "Retrieve the necklace, Steele, Lady Rosalynd. Give my daughter her future."

"We will do our best," Rosalynd said.

As we emerged from the study, I offered my arm to Rosalynd. She hesitated, her gaze holding mine as if seeking reassurance. After I gave her a subtle nod, she slipped her hand into the crook of my elbow.

"Do people ever visit orangeries?" I asked on our way there.

"We do the one at home. It's one of my favorite places to visit during the long winter months. I love the scent, you see."

The orangery turned out to be a wonder. The citrus fruits imbued the space with a pungent but pleasant aroma.

"It is quite aromatic," I murmured, breathing in the heady smell. "So what can these be used for, other than eating of course?"

"Well, lemon oil can be distilled from lemons which makes for a powerful wood shine. Extracts of orange peels are added to perfumes, and limes add flavor to food."

I wasn't surprised by her knowledge, but I was curious about how she'd learned it. "How do you know all this?"

"My brother grows all manners of plants and fruits, mostly to advance the science of botany. He's even an acknowledged expert on poisonous ones."

I stared at her. "Whyever would he study poisons?"

"He finds them fascinating. Scotland Yard regularly consults with him. All manners of poison are used to murder people. When the police suspect one was employed, they turn to him."

Unable to discuss the investigation for fear of being overheard, we spent the remainder of the time in desultory conversation. Close to an hour later, we received word that the coast was clear.

Together we ascended the grand staircase in silence, the soft rustle of her skirts brushing against my side. When we reached the second floor landing, I leaned toward her. "Have you done this sort of thing before, Lady Rosalynd?"

"Breaking and entering? Not precisely. But I'm not unfamiliar with thinking on my feet."

"Good," I murmured, casting a glance down the hallway. "Burkett isn't a man to trifle with. If things go awry, we'll need all the wit and charm you can muster."

"And you, Your Grace? What will you bring to the table?" she asked.

"Let's just say I'm adept at vanishing when the need arises."

Reaching Burkett's door, I tested the handle—locked, as expected. From my pocket, I withdrew a set of tools, the metallic clink breaking the stillness.

"Impressive," Rosalynd whispered, her voice laced with curiosity.

The lock yielded to my hand in seconds. Pushing the door open, I gestured for her to enter ahead of me.

Lord Burkett's air carried the faint scent of cigar smoke, mingling with the bitterness of old paper and brandy. I moved methodically through the space, my movements precise and practiced, while Rosalynd stood by the fireplace, nervously watching the door.

"Anything yet?" she whispered, her voice barely carrying over the faint rustle of papers.

"No," I muttered, my tone tight. "He wouldn't leave the necklace lying about in plain sight."

Frustration bubbled in her gaze, and I knew why. Eleanor's necklace—the one precious possession her family had managed to hold onto—had to be somewhere in this house. Without it, her engagement to Lord Cumberforth would be imperiled. I clenched my hands, determined not to fail her.

A faint sound froze us both. Footsteps. Distinct and deliberate, echoing in the hallway beyond the heavy door.

I straightened, my sharp gaze snapping to hers. "Needham failed to keep Burkett occupied," I murmured.

She nodded in agreement, her gaze darting toward the door.

There was no time to retreat the way we came. I crossed the room in three swift strides and pushed open a connecting door that led into the adjoining chamber.

"Quickly," I urged, holding it open for her.

CHAPTER 10

SCANDALS AND STRATAGEMS

I STEPPED THROUGH behind Steele, only to come to a sudden halt. My breath caught as I took in the scene before me. This was no dressing room as I expected—it was a lady's bedchamber, its walls adorned with soft pastel silks and its air perfumed with lavender and rosewater. A four-poster bed dominated one corner, and a chaise lounge stood near the window, where Lady Burkett herself reclined with a book in hand.

She blinked at us, her expression shifting from confusion to curiosity. "Lady Rosalynd, Your Grace," she said, her tone light with amusement. "To what do I owe the pleasure of this ... unexpected visit?"

Before I could stammer out a reply, the connecting door behind us burst open, slamming against the wall with a thunderous crash. Lord Burkett stormed in, his face flushed with fury.

"What is the meaning of this?" he roared, his gaze darting

between Steele, Lady Burkett, and me. "Lady Rosalynd, what are you doing in my wife's chambers?"

I opened my mouth, but no words came.

As my mind raced for a plausible explanation, Steele spoke, his voice smooth and unruffled despite the volatile situation. "My lord, I must apologize for this intrusion." He slightly inclined his head. "It was not our intention to disturb Lady Burkett."

Lord Burkett's face darkened further. "Not your intention? Then what, pray tell, *was* your intention, skulking about our quarters like common thieves?"

Lady Burkett, who had been watching the exchange with a faint smile, chuckled softly. "Oh, Edward, do calm yourself. Can you not see what's happening here?"

Her husband shot her a bewildered glance. "What on earth are you talking about?"

Coming to her feet, Lady Burkett's eyes sparkled with mischief as she glanced at Steele and me. "It's perfectly obvious," she said, setting her book aside. "Steele and Lady Rosalynd were merely seeking a . . . private moment together."

I gasped, heat rushing to my cheeks. "That is absolutely—"

"Exactly the reason," Steele cut in smoothly, stepping forward to shield me from Burkett's withering glare. "We deeply regret the impropriety, my lady, but I must commend your discretion in understanding the situation."

"Discretion?" Lord Burkett sputtered, his face turning an alarming shade of red. "You expect me to believe—"

Lady Burkett waved a languid hand, cutting him off. "Edward, let it go. Surely you remember the folly of youth?" She cast a sly glance at Steele, her expression one of indulgent amusement. "I would suggest that you both leave now before further misunderstandings arise."

Steele gave her a polite bow, his composure utterly

unshaken. "Thank you, my lady, for your gracious understanding. Come, Lady Rosalynd."

I had no choice but to follow him, my heart pounding with equal parts mortification and outrage. We slipped past Lord Burkett, whose spluttering protests echoed behind us as Steele guided me down the corridor with a firm hand at my elbow.

The moment we were far enough from the bedchamber to avoid being overheard, I whirled on him, yanking my arm free. "You cannot be serious," I hissed, my voice low but venomous. "A *tryst*, Steele? That was the best you could come up with?"

"It wasn't I who suggested it, if you will recall." He raised an eyebrow, his expression maddeningly calm. "And it did work. We managed to extricate ourselves from a sticky situation."

"It did not work!" I exclaimed, incredulous. "You've tarnished my reputation and made me complicit in some sordid fiction!"

"Keep your voice down lest the entire household hears your words."

I blew out a breath.

"Lady Burkett's explanation was better that having Lord Burkett raise an outcry," he said coolly. "Or would you have preferred he discover exactly what we were doing there?"

I glared at him, my hands balling into fists at my sides. "You could have come up with another reason!"

"Such as?"

"We were having a private word with Lady Burkett."

"Regarding what?"

"Fashion."

He chuckled. "With me along? Burkett wouldn't have believed that for a moment." His lips twitched, as though he were suppressing a smile. "Lady Burkett's amusement provided the perfect cover. She practically handed it to us on a silver platter. I merely . . . accepted her interpretation."

"Her 'interpretation' will spread through this house faster than a kitchen fire," I shot back. "By supper, every guest will think I've been cavorting with you in private chambers!"

Steele leaned closer, his voice dropping to a conspiratorial murmur. "Lady Burkett won't spread the tale. I believe we can trust her."

Maybe so, but I couldn't let go of my grievance. "What if she does?"

He tossed a languid hand in the air. "Then let them think what they will. While they're gossiping about us, no one will suspect what we're truly after."

I stared at him, caught between fury and mortification. "That's quite a turnaround from last night, and even this morning, when you warned me about such a thing."

"It would serve a greater purpose. Misdirection is a wonderful strategy."

How could he be so dense? "I have a sister to bring out this season, Your Grace," I hissed out through gritted teeth. "Any scandal that touches me touches her. I cannot afford rumors to be spread about my lack of virtue, especially when they are utterly false."

He suddenly grew serious. "My apologies. I didn't think."

"You wouldn't. Scandals rarely prove detrimental to men even as they destroy women's lives."

He glanced back over his shoulder. "Should I return to Lady Burkett and ask her not to spread the rumor?"

For a few moments, I considered his suggestion. "No. I believe you're correct. She won't say anything." I bit down on my lip. "But her husband might."

"No." He shook his head. "He won't."

"How do you know?"

"I'll have a quiet word with him."

"And what would that word entail?"

"That he might be missing some teeth if he so much as breathes your name."

"Violence never solves anything."

"It's not violence, only the threat of it." He straightened, his expression softening just enough to reveal a flicker of sincerity. "I apologize for making light of what just transpired. I did not mean any harm. But if even the hint of it comes to light, I give you my word I'll do my utmost to repair any damage to your good name."

"Thank you." That was the best I could hope for even if it would do no good. No one would believe him.

"Trust me," he said. "By the time we've solved this mystery, you'll be the heroine of the hour."

"I seek no glory, Steele. I only want Eleanor's necklace found." I pinned a hard gaze on him. "But I promise you this. If you ever put me in such a position again, I'll make sure you pay the price."

"Duly noted, my lady," he said, his tone laced with amusement. As much as I hated to admit it, the sound warmed me. In the next moment, however, he became serious once more. "We need to let Needham know we were not successful."

"Yes." I was not looking forward to that discussion. I'd been so sure we'd find the necklace in Lord Burkett's chamber.

Our walk back to the study was cloaked in silence, the air heavy with unspoken disappointment. We had searched Burkett's quarters thoroughly, but the necklace remained elusive.

Upon arriving, we found Lord Needham pacing the study, his brow furrowed with worry. He looked up as we entered. The flicker of hope in his eyes dimmed at our somber expressions.

"You didn't find it," he said, his voice heavy with resignation.

"No," Steele replied, his tone clipped. "If Burkett has it, he's hidden it well."

Needham sighed and rubbed his temple. "I spoke to Lavinia while you were engaged in your search. You were right. She witnessed Felicity sneaking into Eleanor's room and emerging with a velvet bag in her hand. When she overheard Eleanor telling Cumberforth about the missing necklace, she realized Felicity had stolen it. At that point, she decided to take matters into her own hands and write the blackmail note."

"Why didn't she come to Eleanor or you?" I asked.

"She wanted to claim the glory of finding the necklace."

"Silly chit," Steele exclaimed.

"Yes, she is that," Needham agreed. "She claimed she never intended to act on her threats. She only wanted the necklace returned."

Steele raised an eyebrow. "You believed her?"

"I don't know," Needham admitted. "Lavinia thrives on drama, but she also values her place in society. Ruining her cousin's name would tarnish hers as well."

Before we could delve further, the sound of voices filtered in from the hallway. Felicity and the church party had returned, their laughter incongruous with the tension weighing on the duke, Needham, and me.

"I'll see everyone retires to their rooms to prepare for supper," Needham said in a weary voice. "We could all use a moment to gather ourselves."

As the guests dispersed, Steele stepped closer to Needham. "We can't let this fester any longer. Issue an invitation to everyone involved to meet here at seven. Lavinia, Burkett, Felicity—anyone with a stake in this matter. It's time to get to the truth."

Needham nodded. "You're right."

Steele reached out to press Lord Needham's shoulder in a show of support. "We'll confront them together."

I glanced at Steele, noting the determination etched into his features. Despite my lingering irritation with him, I couldn't deny his resolve. Tonight, one way or another, we would uncover the truth and restore Eleanor's necklace whatever it took.

CHAPTER 11

RESTORING THE NECKLACE

*A*T THE TIME AGREED UPON, the duke and I followed Lord Needham into his study. Once more I was struck by the solemn majesty of the room. The scent of pipe tobacco hung faintly in the air, mingling with the musty aroma of aged books lining the oak-paneled walls. It was a fitting stage for the drama that awaited us—a drama whose tension was almost palpable before we even crossed the threshold.

Inside, the atmosphere was thick with unspoken accusations. Eleanor sat rigid on a chaise, her hands folded tightly in her lap. Her eyes flitted nervously between her cousin Lavinia, who looked as though she were about to deliver a scathing proclamation, and Lord Cumberforth, who stood nearby with a composed yet wary expression. Across the room, Felicity shifted uncomfortably, her gaze fixed firmly on the intricate carpet beneath her feet. By the fireplace sat

Lord Burkett, his stern visage as unreadable as a granite statue.

"Good evening," Lord Needham said to those assembled there, his tone somber. The duke and I took our places near the hearth. While he stood, I chose to sit, both of us prepared to observe before speaking.

"What the devil are we doing here, Needham?" Lord Burkett demanded, his voice brimming with fury, his eyes narrowing in barely restrained anger.

Lord Needham met the outburst head-on, his stance unyielding, his tone as steely as his resolve. "My daughter Eleanor's diamond necklace has gone missing, Burkett. As you can imagine, it has caused her great distress. But the implications reach far beyond the theft itself. There are deeper truths at stake. They will all be revealed here tonight no matter where they lead."

"I wonder," Lavinia began, her voice honeyed with venom, "if by deeper truths you mean the unsavory rumors surrounding Edwin." The crimson feathers that adorned her head trembled. She just couldn't help herself, scandalmonger that she was. "I, for one, refuse to stand idly by while—"

"Enough, Lavinia," Needham snapped, his sharp tone cutting her off. "This is no time for unfounded accusations."

Unfounded, perhaps, but not forgotten. The tension in the room thickened, and I braced myself for the storm that was about to break.

Just then, the door swung open with a bang, startling us all. Needham's younger brother, Martin, strode in, his face dark with anger. Trailing behind him was Edwin, his normally composed demeanor replaced by a nervous pallor.

"Martin," Needham said. "You shouldn't be here."

"On the contrary, brother, this is exactly where I need to be." He glanced at Edwin with a father's fond gaze. "Edwin has told me everything. I will not have his reputation dragged through the mud by petty gossip and lies. I will not allow my son's honor to be sullied!" Martin declared, his voice echoing in the confined space.

"Petty gossip, is it?" Lavinia stood, her cheeks flushed with indignation. "Everyone knows the truth, Uncle Martin."

"You know nothing!" Martin thundered, silencing her with a glare. "Edwin is my son, legitimate in every sense. My wife never betrayed me. Her virtue is unimpeachable."

I came to my feet and stepped forward. "Forgive me for what I'm about to say, sir. I only wish to arrive at the truth. A member of your family doubts Edwin's parentage. How did this misunderstanding arise?" I asked, keeping my tone gentle.

Martin Needham hesitated, glancing at Edwin before speaking. "My dear wife wished to travel to France, the land of her mother's birth. She was two months before her confinement and in stout health, so her physician approved the trip. But as soon as we arrived in a small French village, her pains started. Edwin was born, healthy but small. My dear Charlotte did not survive. I returned to England a broken man, with my wife's body in a casket, a babe, and a wet nurse I paid to feed my son. It took me years to recover. I never stopped grieving for her. I saw no reason to discuss such a private matter. I had no idea my silence would lead to such cruelty." His eyes narrowed into slits as he gazed at Lavinia. Anger and disdain for his niece fairly pulsed out of him. "I won't tell your father what you have done, but you're no longer welcomed in my home."

"What I have done?" Lavinia cried out. "Your daughter stole Eleanor's necklace. What punishment will you visit upon her?"

Felicity's gaze continued to be glued to the carpet even as the color on her face rose.

"I will deal with her. It will not be pretty."

"Thank you, Mister Needham," I said. "I'm sorry you had to relive your pain."

His eyes wet with tears, Edwin placed a hand on his father's shoulder. "Father."

How anyone could have thought they were not father and son was beyond me. They shared the same height, eye color, and aquiline nose.

It took a moment for Martin Needham to compose himself. When he finally did, Edwin led him to a solitary corner where they could quietly converse.

Into the tension-laden silence, a knock sounded on the door.

"Enter," Lord Needham declared.

The Needham butler strode purposefully into the room. "Begging your pardon, Milord. Lady Burkett wishes to have a word."

I glanced at Steele, fearful of what she would say.

"Have her come in."

All eyes turned to the doorway as Lady Burkett swept into the room with regal authority. In her hands, she carried a small velvet bag. The butler left, closing the door quietly behind her.

"Good evening," she announced, her tone brisk and businesslike. "I'm sorry to interrupt but I believe I have something that belongs to Lady Eleanor."

She approached her son's fiancée, opening the bag to retrieve the missing necklace. The diamonds sparkled like stars, their brilliance undiminished by their mysterious disappearance.

"My necklace!" Eleanor gasped, rising to her feet. "But where—how did you come by it?"

Lady Burkett's expression hardened. "Among my husband's possessions," she said, each word a dagger.

THE STOLEN SPARKLER

The collective gasp was nearly deafening. Lord Burkett shifted uncomfortably but said nothing.

"You have nothing to say for yourself?" Lady Burkett demanded of him, her voice cold as winter frost. "Shall I explain it for you? You orchestrated this theft, hoping to sabotage our son's engagement. By depriving Lady Eleanor of her dowry, you intended to force Stephen to break the betrothal and marry the heiress of your choosing. Did you not?"

All eyes turned to Lord Burkett, whose stern composure finally cracked under the weight of the accusation.

"I acted in his best interest," he muttered, though his words rang hollow.

"No. You acted in your own interest," Lady Burkett snapped. "Don't worry. I won't air our dirty linen in public, however much I wish to do so."

"I have no such compunction, Mother," Lord Cumberforth said, stepping forward to confront his father.

"Best not, dear." She glanced pointedly at Lavinia. "We've already provided enough grist for the mill of the scandalmonger amongst us."

Lavinia's face flushed bright red.

Lady Burkett glanced pointedly at her husband. "You've interfered enough, Edward. This engagement will proceed, and you will not stand in its way again. Do I make myself clear?"

Lord Burkett opened his mouth, but the fiery glint in his wife's eyes silenced him.

I stood, sensing the need to move the conversation to a resolution. "With the necklace returned and the truth revealed, I trust we can move forward in peace," I said. "Eleanor, are you satisfied with this outcome?"

Eleanor nodded, her face flushed with relief. "I am."

"And you, Lord Cumberforth?"

He took Eleanor's hand, his expression tender. "I could not be more pleased."

The butler, with the seemingly perfect timing only the best staff possessed, knocked and entered once more. "My lord," he announced, "supper is served."

As the group filed out of the study, I caught Lady Burkett's eye. She offered me the faintest of nods—an acknowledgment of a battle hard-won. It seemed the evening, once poised for disaster, would end on a bright note.

CHAPTER 12

◈

THE CHRISTMAS BALL

THE FESTIVE HUM of the Christmas Ball enveloped the grand hall as I surveyed the scene. The glittering chandeliers bathed the assembled guests in a golden glow as the orchestra's waltz swelled with a spirited charm. At the heart of the spectacle stood Eleanor, resplendent in her restored diamond necklace. Its brilliance caught the light with every turn of her graceful head, drawing admiring glances and murmurs of approval. She seemed lighter now, the weight of the weekend's turmoil lifted, her joy evident in her radiant smile as she spoke with her fiancé, Lord Cumberforth.

I approached her, my lips curving into a warm smile. "Congratulations, my dear friend. Your engagement is now official."

Her face lit up with a mixture of joy and relief before offering me a warm embrace. "Thank you, Rosalynd. Thank you for everything. Without you, my necklace would still be missing, and who knows what might have happened?"

I chuckled softly, shaking my head. "You should be thanking Lady Burkett, not me. She's the one who discovered it."

Eleanor laughed, the sound bright and unrestrained. "Oh, but if you hadn't burst into her chambers and unsettled her, she might never have suspected something was amiss. She confessed to me that after your visit, she searched her husband's room. That's when she found the necklace."

I raised a brow, clearly amused. "I suppose a bit of dramatic flair has its uses. Speaking of drama, I couldn't help but notice Felicity's conspicuous absence tonight."

Eleanor leaned closer, her voice dropping to a conspiratorial whisper. "Uncle Martin forbade her from attending. She's upstairs right now, packing her bags. He's threatening to send her to a nunnery."

My eyes widened in mock astonishment. "A nunnery? Felicity? I can't quite picture her taking vows of poverty and chastity."

We both burst into laughter, our mirth drawing a few curious glances from nearby guests.

Eleanor dabbed at her eyes with a lace handkerchief, still chuckling. "Neither can I. I imagine the nuns would be in for quite the shock."

"And Felicity," I added with a sly grin, "wouldn't last a week."

Our laughter lingered, a shared moment of levity amidst an evening full of new beginnings and restored harmony.

"Lavinia appears somewhat subdued." I nodded toward Eleanor's cousin who was sitting on the fringes among the wallflowers.

"I had a quiet word with her."

"Oh?" I asked, my curiosity piqued.

"I told her if she spread any rumors about anyone in our family, I would see to it that everyone knew what she'd been up to in the orangery."

"Pray tell," I urged.

"She accosted one of our footmen. By the time our housekeeper interceded, she almost had his trousers off him."

I giggled. Oh, my."

"Poor Phillip was so embarrassed he didn't know what to do."

"Which one is Phillip?"

"He's standing there, by the refreshments table." She nodded in that direction.

Philip was a strapping young man, with a full head of blonde hair, and the body of an Adonis. "Well, at least she has good taste."

"Father has written a letter to Uncle Wilford informing him of her activities with a strong recommendation to marry her off as quickly as possible before she disgraces herself."

"Does she have any suitors?" I asked, glancing back at Eleanor.

"Lord Waddling."

"He must be fifty five years old if he's a day!"

"And looking for a young wife to warm his bed."

"Poor Lavinia," I would never wish an old, randy husband on anyone.

"She brought it on herself."

Even as we laughed the duke caught my eye. In seemingly predatory fashion, he was approaching the refreshment table where Lord Burkett stood. What could he possibly want to discuss with him?

∼

Lord Burkett's hawklike gaze darted across the room, perhaps seeking allies in his thwarted schemes. Knowing his type, I anticipated he might attempt further sabotage. It was time to put a stop to that.

"Burkett," I greeted him evenly, my voice low enough to avoid attracting attention from those nearby.

He turned. "Steele. To what do I owe this pleasure?" The hate in his eyes belied the polite greeting.

I stepped closer, my tone soft but pointed. "Let us dispense with pleasantries. The engagement between Cumberforth and Lady Eleanor is to proceed. I trust you'll play the doting father-in-law tonight, offering them your hearty congratulations?"

Burkett's lips thinned. "I've already done more than I ought to. This engagement does little to—"

I narrowed my gaze and gritted my teeth. "If you're thinking of further impediments, I assure you they'll backfire. Your machinations with the necklace theft were a disgrace. Were I to make them public—and I will, should you waver—your reputation would suffer irreparable harm. That would hardly be in your or your son's interest."

Burkett bristled, his fists tightening at his sides, but I pressed on. "A word of advice: sometimes retreat is the wiser course. Offer your blessings tonight, and I'll consider the matter closed. Fail to do so, and you'll find I have a long memory and a relentless sense of duty."

A flicker of something—defeat, perhaps—crossed his face. He knew he had no choice. With a curt nod, he muttered, "Very well, Steele. You've made yourself clear."

"Oh, one more thing. If you even so much as breathe Lady Rosalynd's name in the future, it won't be your reputation that will suffer. A certain part of your anatomy will pay the price."

"You wouldn't dare!" Burkett sputtered.

"Au contraire, you *branleur de cheval*. If you don't believe me, ask Collingsford." The knave in question had suffered a serious mishap after he'd seduced an innocent young lady.

Burkett turned white as a sheet. "Collingsford? I heard he fell off his horse—"

"Yes, that's what he claimed," I drawled. "The truth is much uglier. Rather unfortunate, don't you think?" The accident left Collingsford unable to perform the most vital of male functions. Gossip being what it was, of course, everyone knew.

Leaving him in a state of horror, I allowed my steps to carry me back into the glittering swirl of the ball. It was not long before Burkett approached the happy couple, his smile strained but serviceable as he shook his son's hand and clapped him on the shoulder. Eleanor beamed at Burkett, entirely unaware of the coercion behind her future father-in-law's apparent change of heart.

Satisfied with my efforts, I allowed my gaze to wander until it landed on Lady Rosalynd. She stood by the edge of the dance floor, watching the couples glide past with an air of quiet observation. Her gold gown suited her perfectly, as did the thoughtful expression on her face.

It was time for a different sort of negotiation.

I made my way to her side and bowed slightly. "Lady Rosalynd, may I have the honor of this dance?"

She turned to me, her lips curving into a smile that held more amusement than agreement. "I fear I'm not in the mood for dancing tonight, Your Grace. Perhaps we might promenade instead?"

"An excellent alternative," I said, offering my arm. She placed her hand lightly on it, and we began a leisurely circuit of the room.

The soft murmur of conversation surrounded us, but we spoke quietly, our words meant only for each other. "A rather eventful weekend," I remarked.

"To say the least," she replied with a rueful smile. "I'm glad we solved the mystery, but I can't help feeling I didn't truly get to enjoy the festivities. There was no time to celebrate properly."

I raised a brow. "And how do you propose to rectify that once you return home?"

Her expression brightened. "There's plenty to keep me occupied. We will celebrate our own holiday festivities, of course. And with the new year, we will have a new purpose. My sister Chrissie is to make her debut this season. We'll be planning her wardrobe—evening gowns, cloaks, walking dresses, hats, footwear. No detail will be overlooked. Fashion plates from Paris will be perused endlessly."

I shook my head. "Please, spare me the rest. The intricacies of lace and ribbons are far beyond my comprehension."

"And what about you, Your Grace?" she asked, her eyes sparkling with curiosity. "What responsibilities await you?"

I adopted a mock-solemn expression. "As a leading light in the House of Lords, I'll be drafting proposals for legislation. It's a task of monumental importance."

"Is that so?" she replied. "Then I hope you'll take note of the Society for the Advancement of Women. We're submitting a proposal advocating for woman suffrage."

For a moment, I considered her words, uncertain how to respond. My hesitation must have been evident, but Rosalynd, ever perceptive, did not press me. Instead, she allowed the topic to linger in the air, its significance undeniable.

"Perhaps," I said at last, "the world is changing more quickly than some of us can grasp."

She smiled softly, as though acknowledging both my doubt and the possibility of growth. "Perhaps."

We continued our promenade in companionable silence, the hum of the ball a pleasant backdrop to our thoughts. The events of the weekend had revealed much—secrets, schemes, and a shared determination to set things right. I should be satisfied—and I was. But I couldn't help but feel there should be more.

As the evening drew to a close and the strains of the orchestra signaled the final dance, I turned to her. "Now that we've solved the mystery, perhaps we can look forward to simpler pleasures."

She tilted her head, a teasing glint in her eyes. "Simpler, Your Grace? I can't imagine you'd settle for anything so mundane."

I laughed, a genuine sound that surprised even me. "Perhaps not. But I find the prospect of certain complications rather appealing."

Her cheeks flushed faintly, but she met my gaze steadily. "Then I suppose we'll see where those complications lead."

As the final notes of the waltz faded into the night, the room seemed to glow with warmth and cheer. The mystery was solved, the stolen necklace restored, and the future of one young couple secured. Yet, as I bid goodnight to Lady Rosalynd, I couldn't shake the feeling that somehow, someway our lives would intertwine once more.

∽

DID you enjoy THE STOLEN SPARKLER? If you did, you may wish to read **A MURDER IN MAYFAIR**, Book 1 in the Rosalynd and Steele Mysteries.

LONDON. 1889. **Lady Rosalynd Rosehaven.** Fierce advocate of women's causes. As guardian of her brothers and sisters, she considers herself a spinster. **The Duke of Steele.** A leader in the House of Lords. After the tragic death of his wife, he's sworn to remain a widower. Although they once worked together to find a stolen necklace, their paths are not likely to cross again.

But when her cousin is suspected of her husband's murder and the duke's brother is implicated as well, Steele suggests they join forces to investigate the killing. Such an alliance would upset Rosalynd's well-ordered life. She'd found the duke arrogant, aloof, and . . . fascinating. However, she has no choice but to accept his offer. Proving her cousin's innocence takes precedence over her nonsensical misgivings.

As they track down clues from the opulent mansions of Mayfair to the sordid streets of St. Giles, they don't lack for suspects. Few had a good opinion of the victim who was considered a swindler, a card sharp, and worse. When a clue comes to light that leads to her cousin's arrest, Rosalynd embarks on a dangerous course. Can the duke stop her mad quest before she pays with her life?

From the pen of *USA Today* Bestselling Author **Magda Alexander** comes this captivating Victorian historical mystery. Fans of the Bow Street Duchess Mysteries and the Angus Brodie & Mikaela Forsythe series will love **A MURDER IN MAYFAIR**, Book 1 in The Rosalynd and Steele Mysteries.

CAST OF CHARACTERS

The Rosehaven Family

Cosmos, Earl of Rosehaven
Lady Rosalynd Rosehaven, sister to Cosmos
Ladies Chrysanthemum ("Chrissie"), Holly, Ivy, Laurel and Petunia (sisters to Rosalynd and Cosmos)
William and Foxglove ("Fox") (Brothers to Cosmos and Rosalynd)

The Duke of Steele, a law unto himself, a leading light at the House of Lords

The Needham Family

Lord Needham, an earl, master of Needham Hall
Lady Eleanor Needham, Lord Needham's daughter, friend to Lady Rosalynd
Martin Needham (Lord Needham's brother)
Felicity Needham (Martin's daughter)
Edwin Needham (Martin's son)

CAST OF CHARACTERS

Lavinia Needham (Lord Needham's niece)
Alistair Needham (Lord Needham's nephew, heir to the Needham title and estate, brother to Lavinia)

The Burkett Family

Lord Burkett, a marquis
Lady Burkett, his wife
Lord Stephen Cumberforth, their son

Other Notable Characters

Tilly, Lady Rosalynd's Maid

This book is a work of fiction. All names, characters, locations, and incidents are products of the author's imagination or have been used fictitiously. Any resemblance to actual persons living or dead, locales, or events is entirely coincidental.

Copyright © 2024 by Amalia Villalba

All rights reserved.

The uploading, scanning, and distribution of this book in any form or by any means—including but not limited to electronic, mechanical, photocopying, recording, or otherwise—without the permission of the copyright holder is illegal and punishable by law. Please purchase only authorized editions of this work, and do not participate in or encourage electronic piracy of copyrighted materials. Your support of the author's rights is appreciated.

ISBN-13: (eBook) 978-1-943321-38-4

ISBN-13 (Print) 978-1-943321-42-1

Made in United States
Orlando, FL
22 July 2025